DEVIL'S BREATH

GREG F. GIFUNE

JOURNALSTONE
YOUR LINK TO ARTIST TALENT

JournalStone books may be ordered through booksellers or by contacting:
JournalStone
www.journalstone.com

The views expressed in this work are solely those of the authors and do not necessarily reflect the views of the publisher, and the publisher hereby disclaims any responsibility for them.

ISBN: 978-1-947654-91-4 (sc)
ISBN: 978-1-947654-92-1 (ebook)

JournalStone rev. date: April 19, 2019
2nd Edition
1st Edition DarkFuse, 2015

Library of Congress Control Number: 2019934276

Printed in the United States of America

Cover Design: Zach McCain
Interior Layout: Jess Landry

Proofread by Sean Leonard

For Frank Scala

DEVIL'S BREATH

"It is better to burn than to disappear."
—Albert Camus, *The Stranger*

1

IT'S A TERRIBLE THING to know terrible things.

* * *

The mirror is oval and dirty, smudged and smeared with grime. Neglected, like the old abandoned building in which it hangs, it provides a barely discernable reflection of the young woman standing before it. Her face is blurred and horrific, her eyes little more than empty black sockets, her hair tight to the sides of her head and her mouth and chin concealed in shadows and filth.

Outside, fog rolls, encapsulates the world, surrounds us, creeping slowly closer like a sentient being, absorbing everything and everyone in its path. What few windows exist here are blown out and tattered, jagged wounds bleeding mist-filled nightmares from minds long broken.

"Do you know where we are?"

"No," I answer, our voices blasphemy in silence so treacherous.

"Do you know what's happening?"

I shake my head no, and despite my terror, turn away from her and seek out the closest window instead. Through the thick fog, traces of a town peer at me from a great distance, the buildings and skyline—everything—a dull, oppressive, barely perceptible blanket of gray separated by a vast stretch of equally ashen placid ocean.

"Are we asleep?" the young woman asks, distracting me from the ghosts.

Rather than answer, I glance down at my hand. It clutches something shiny and sharp. A straight razor, its blade reflecting back a distorted and elongated version of myself, like some altered alien being bent and gliding across time and space, warped by a universe gone mad.

I turn back to her, perhaps for answers.

"There's something wrong," she says. "Something inside us."

It is then that I realize it's her reflection in the dirty mirror I'm looking at.

"They're coming," she says.

Her lips do not move when she speaks.

"We shouldn't be here," I tell her, think, or only dream.

Something overhead catches my attention. The ceiling is dark but looks almost liquid, undulating and swelling as if alive. Spiders. It is covered with thousands of plump black spiders that threaten to pour down on us in a mutant rain.

"Do it," someone whispers. Someone else. Some...other.

I grip the razor tighter, bring it to my face and slash it quickly and savagely across my cheek then back again, butchering my flesh in arcing swings.

Something moves behind us, shifts and disturbs the pile of broken bloody bones gathered at our feet. And somewhere not so very far away, someone begins to scream.

*   *   *

Early morning seemed a good time to die.

I'd known hard times in my life but suicide never occurred to me in any real sense. Yet here it was, staring me right in the face. Forty-six years on this earth and this was what it had all come to, what it ultimately amounted to. It began as a dull murmur I paid little attention to, but the inevitability of it gathered strength slowly. Like a stranger seen from a great distance coming up over a horizon blurred by heat and dust, it gradually evolved into something tangible, recognizable and fully realized. I could no longer dismiss it as the conceptual musings of an emotionally exhausted mind, and unlike before, when I'd been able to debate the pros and cons in my head for hours on end then eventually dismiss the entire thing as ridiculous, the more I thought about it, the more sense it made. The alternative, to continue on as I'd been doing, seemed pointless, though a flicker of instinctual desire remained. Some primal part of me was still fighting for survival, clinging to an underlying need to fight this off like the enemy it was. This led me to believe that perhaps deep down I was flirting with the concept of death rather than the reality. But death was anything but conceptual. There was nothing more literal.

Earlier that morning, suffering from one of the worst hangovers I'd ever had, I stood before the mirror over the bathroom sink, brushed my teeth and stared into my own dark eyes as if hoping for a reprieve. Oddly, I'd seen that same desperation in quiet moments over the last few months, and it too had gone unanswered. It was then that I knew for sure no pardon was forthcoming. There would be no rescue, and therefore no escape, and accompanying that strange epiphany was an acceptance and peace I hadn't felt prior. I celebrated with a swig of Listerine.

It's okay, I told myself. *Just get it over with.*

It was time. I didn't understand how I knew that exactly, but I did, and with an eerie and unexpected calm, I cleaned and tidied my little cottage then washed the dishes and put them away, stacking each one neatly in the cupboard. Once finished, I showered, shaved, combed my hair and dressed in a pair of black chinos, black shoes and a black shirt. After all, I was going to a funeral, might as well dress for it.

I'd already decided not to pen a note. There was no reasonable explanation for what I was about to do and no flowery goodbye letter was going to change that.

Besides, who'd read it anyway? Some paramedic, the cops, maybe the landlord? Instead, I slid into a chair at the two-person kitchen table and thought about when I was a kid, and how I had no idea then that one day I'd be sitting at this table mere moments from taking my own life. I tried to summon pleasant memories but they refused to cooperate, so after a minute or two I rose from the chair, walked to the bathroom and retrieved the straight razor from the edge of the sink. I'd placed it there earlier so I wouldn't have to go looking for it once the time came. Glimpsing myself in the mirror, I realized this would be the last time I'd see my reflection.

I gazed deeply into my own eyes for what seemed a very long time, then forced myself back to the kitchen area and again sat at the table. At first I'd considered taking pills, I still had nearly a full bottle of heavy-duty pain meds from when I'd wrenched my back at work several months before, but overdoses often failed. I'd heard too many stories of people swallowing a boatload of narcotics and still surviving. I had a shotgun and pistol in the bedroom closet, and while shooting myself was probably the best route—quick, easy and final—there was also the small but very real risk of not finishing the job properly. All I had to do was move at the last second and I could end up a mangled vegetable instead of dead. The only way to get it done for sure was to open my veins. I'd slash my wrists quick and deep and just bleed out. I'd lose so much blood so quickly that by the time it hit me I'd already be drifting off to wherever the hell I was going. Messy and initially painful to be sure, it was also as close to fail-safe as I was likely to get.

The steadiness of my hand surprised me. I'd assumed when the time came my hands would be shaking and I'd be afraid. But that wasn't the case. Even with a horrible hangover thrown into the mix, I'd never felt calmer or more at ease. The silver blade caught the light from the ceiling fixture, reflecting it with curious beauty. I placed the razor in front of me, then unbuttoned my shirtsleeves and neatly rolled them up to my elbows. Studying the blue veins along my wrists, I reached for the blade, trying my best to prepare for the spurt once I made the cut. I decided to slash my left wrist first. Then I'd transfer the razor as quickly as possible to my other hand and slash the right before I lost strength or nerve, or fell into shock.

Suddenly cognizant of everything around me, I drew a deep breath.

Should I pray? Was anyone listening? Did it even matter?

The world and all my senses seemed heightened. I could hear traffic in the distance, the rattle and hum of the air conditioner in the window, the blood rushing through my veins, my heart thudding in my chest, the slow and steady cadence of my breath. I could feel the moisture in my eyes with each blink, feel my eyelashes flutter and brush against each other, and taste—I could taste my saliva and the remnants of mouthwash in a way I never had before—even that was sharper and more defined. The visions of my childhood that had eluded me earlier revealed themselves in living color, drifting past my mind's eye. Scenes from a failed life, *my* life, followed, yet even then I still saw myself like I'd once been: young, healthy, strong and happy. That all seemed so very long ago now, and it gradually faded, swallowed into darkness with all the rest.

The world was burning all around me, and nothing seemed real, yet this was harsh and unbridled reality at its heightened finest. Perhaps its worst. Then again, like nearly everything else, maybe there wasn't a hell of a lot of difference.

I closed my eyes. A tear trickled the length of my face.

A strange sound echoed through my mind as if from far away. I wiped my face and eyes with the back of my free hand, tightened my grip on the razor with the other and listened a moment. What the hell was that noise?

Knocking. Someone was knocking on a door. My door.

No, I thought. *No one's knocking. It's in your head, some primal defense mechanism triggered to distract you from the task at hand.*

My cottage was one of several along a partially wooded bluff over-looking the ocean. But for Mrs. Muir next door, who was too elderly and decrepit to make the walk from her place to mine, and Albert Smithee, my landlord and a night owl who lived with his girlfriend Carla in the cottage on the other side of mine and was likely still asleep, the other cottages were seasonal rentals occupied by tourists.

No one's at the door, I told myself. *Stay focused.*

I looked to the blade, so sharp and deadly. *Do it.*

Strange. Was that my voice in my head, or someone else's?

The knocking came again, louder this time and with more persis-tence, the old door rattling against the onslaught. Someone was defi-nitely there.

Maybe someone selling something, I thought.

I waited, hoping they might give up and go away, but the knocking continued.

A shuddering swept through me as a distant and ethereal voice drifted through my mind.

Come and see, it said. *Come and see…*

There then gone, it left me shaken. I put the blade aside and stood up. My legs were shaky, so I took a moment to collect myself.

When I first opened the door, I thought perhaps I'd already gone through with it, and had entered a bizarre dream state or moment of madness, lingering between life and death on a slowly unraveling thread, because what stood before me was so startling I couldn't com-prehend it. I glanced behind me to the table, partly as an excuse to look away from what had knocked on my door, and partly to see if I'd collapsed there and begun bleeding out all over the kitchen.

My entire body trembling, I turned back to the door and looked directly into my own eyes. The person that had knocked was me, or someone that looked just like me, some long-lost twin or doppelgänger, bloodied about the face and neck, flesh slashed with deep gashes from what was likely a razor.

I stood there staring at myself. Neither of us said a word.

This other me looked as troubled as I was, but seemed unconcerned or perhaps even unaware of his horrific wounds. He gazed at me as I did him, mouth open and eyes wide.

Drifting into the insanity I was sure had taken me, I slowly reached out and touched my ravaged face, pressing my fingers deep into the wet and sticky wounds. My stomach clenched and I was certain I'd vomit. But I didn't, and neither did I.

The phone began to ring. I followed the sound, looking back over my shoulder a second time.

When I turned back, the other me was gone.

I stepped outside, looked around, my head spinning and my heart racing. Had I hallucinated just then? Had I been dreaming? Was I still?

The phone continued to ring.

Pulse pounding in time with the new drumbeat in my temples, I went back inside, locked the door and fell against it, my mind a jumble of confusion. Just then, my hangover decided to attack my stomach. It gurgled and clenched, shooting bile into the base of my throat. I winced and choked it back down.

I returned to the table, leaned against it so as not to collapse and considered the remnants of a fate I was so sure awaited me only moments before. Memories of the razor and my heightened senses circled me.

Had the knock on my door come even a few seconds later I'd already be dead.

The phone, with its incessant ringing, brought me back.

Pulling a bottle from the cupboard, I tossed the cap aside and took a long swig, the liquor burning its way into my already upset stomach.

I staggered about a moment, my hangover chiseling away at my temples now with a small pickax. I ran my hands over my body, as if to make sure I was still intact, still there, still real, then noticed the razor on the kitchen table.

I inspected my wrists. No slashes.

The phone, I thought, *the goddamn phone.* Finally finding my way over to it, I read the ID. My father.

I wasn't sure how much more I could handle, so I considered letting it go to voicemail. But my father was seventy-three years old and lived alone. Despite the fact that our relationship at the best of times was virtually nonexistent, when he called, I felt an obligation to answer it. Or maybe I just wanted the fucking thing to stop ringing.

"Stan," he growled once I answered. "For Christ's sake, take your time answering the phone, glad it's not an emergency."

"I was in the other room," I said through a sigh. "What can I do for you, Pop?"

"The other room? You live in a shoebox."

"There some reason for this call?"

"You watch your tone with me, boy."

His speech was slurred, which meant he was already drunk. Since I had alcohol on my breath, at first I thought I shouldn't judge him. Then I remembered who he was and went right ahead. "You drinking already?"

"That's none of your goddamn business. I'm a grown man, I do what I want."

"I'm just on my way out the door," I told him. "What do you need?"

"I don't answer to you."

"Yeah, I got it, forget I asked. What's up?"

"I need to talk to you, the hell you think?" What began as a slight cough quickly turned into a gurgling hack, and was followed by a loud spitting sound, then a violent intake of breath. "Christ," he groaned. "These fucking lungs of mine."

"You all right?"

"No, I'm not fucking *all right*. It sound to you like I'm *all right*?"

I put the bottle down and tightened my grip on the phone with the other, fantasizing it was his neck all the while. "Smoking those cigars again?"

"Never stopped."

"Dr. Apte told you to—"

"I stopped going to that quack," he snapped. "*Apte*, what the hell kind of name is that? Whatever happened to regular American names?"

"There's no such thing as American names."

"Don't start that politically correct liberal retard bullshit with me, boy. *Apte* can kiss my furry white ass. What the hell's he know anyway?"

"He's a doctor."

"Yeah, from India. That country's a bucket of shit. Please, I wouldn't let one of those people treat my fucking cat." He coughed again. "What I'm saying is it shouldn't be that big of a deal to find an American doctor. Maybe you can find a broad, but who wants some skirt for a doctor? How the hell am I supposed to take a girl doctor seriously when I know she puts her legs or ass in the air and gets fucked? Come on, I'm supposed to listen to *her*? I want a broad fiddling with my nuts and sticking a finger up my ass, I'll hire a hooker."

Visions haunted me, pulling me back.

"Anyway," he went on, "besides them it's nothing but a bunch of curry-gobblers and slant-eyed gooks nowadays. Goddamn disgrace."

At least that was something my father knew about. He'd taken being a disgrace to heights few imagined, much less achieved. "Pop, I got shit to do, what do you want?"

"I need you to come by the house."

I ran a hand through my hair. It came back damp with perspiration. I still felt light-headed, confused and frightened. What the hell had just happened? What the hell *was* happening?

"Hey, you even listening to me, boy?"

"Yeah, I—sorry, I—what do you need me to come by for?"

"It's important."

"Needs to be, Pop, it's not like you're right around the corner."

"It's an hour drive, stop acting like I'm on the other side of the world."
If only.

"Want to give me a hint?" I asked, keeping an eye on the door.

"Better to sit down and talk about it like men."

"Yeah, okay. Let me get back to you, not sure what my schedule looks like for the next few days yet."

"Oh, sorry to bother you, Senator Falk. Your *schedule*, are you shitting me? You work at a diner, not the Pentagon. Must be so stressful and hectic, being a dish-cleansing engineer and all. Try doing my job for forty-plus years. Busting my ass ten, twelve hours a day in construction, a working man, a *real* man doing *real* work. And here you are, my son— my only goddamn son, my only goddamn child—with dishpan hands and too busy to come see his father. Jesus, Mary and Joseph, what'd I do to get so lucky, huh? Pride, I'm just bursting with it over here."

Rather than respond, I focused instead on loosening my grip before the phone shattered in my hand. Like always, the sound of his voice brought memories flooding back, all of them bad. Corrupt, foul and re-pellent, just like my old man. I shook my head, hoping it might ward them off. It nearly worked.

"Today," he pressed. "This morning. Leave now, understand?"

"I'll call you back." I disconnected before he could say anything else.

We all find ways to exercise power and control when we can, however contemptible. When it came to my old man, I grabbed both whenever I could, and by whatever means available. I'd go see the miserable sonofa-bitch and find out what he wanted at some point before the day was over, but it'd be when I was damn good and ready.

Right now, I had other things to worry about.

"Bad dreams," I muttered.

The razor on the table sat pristine and unused, shiny with contempt.

At least for now, death would have to wait.

2

LOCATED AT THE END of the main drag in town, The American Dream Diner & Grill was anything but dreamy. More a big tin can and a run-down eyesore from yesteryear that hadn't been particularly well maintained, it fit right in amidst the rest of the dying summer tourist trap village that was Sunset, Massachusetts. I'd worked there nearly a year, and being a dependable and hardworking employee, got along well with most of the staff. Since patience had never been my strong suit, I achieved this by keeping to myself, coming in, doing my job and going home. This also allowed me to tolerate the overbearing owner and cook, Demetrius, a Greek that screamed at everyone in broken English despite having lived in the country for decades. Though thankless, it was steady work with few challenges and even fewer hassles, and that's exactly what I needed. It was about all I could handle. Though I thought I'd seen the last of the diner, there was no reason to miss work at this point. Apparently I'd be sticking around for a while, so I'd need the money anyway.

Several hours into my shift, I loaded the last stack of filthy dishes into the industrial washer and dropped the hood, releasing a rush of steamed heat into the air. The diner was hopping, and I'd been busy in back washing dishes and stacking clean ones without a break for quite a while. It always amazed me the amount of food people wasted. The amounts I'd scrape from plates into the garbage before loading the washer was often startling. Maybe it was because the food wasn't that great. Maybe it's because half the night patrons were either drunk or high or both or in a hurry to go do something else. Regardless, pondering such things served as a useful distraction until my shift was over.

Per usual, the tile floor was sticky and stained, and the typical nauseating smells of grease and hideous food combinations lingered in the air, on my hands and apron and seeped into my pores. Some nights it took hours to get those smells off me, and only a long, hot shower did the trick. Like most nights, I spent my shift distracted, the actual mechanics of the job set to automatic pilot. I could pull a double with my eyes closed, and often, when I found my shift over, I'd have virtually no memory of it. It was mindless, repetitive work, which was precisely what I liked about it. But I was even more distracted than usual. I couldn't shake the memory of the nightmare I'd had—if that's what it was—of seeing a physically mutilated version of myself at the door. I'd knocked at precisely the right time. Was there a deeper meaning behind the timing of this visitation, or was it only coincidence? Had I fallen asleep or into some sort of trance, only to be torn from it by hallucinations and bad dreams?

After the call from my father, I decompressed as best I could and considered just how close I'd come to ending it all. It still seemed the best option for me, but I couldn't check out yet, not with this mystery hanging over my head. Were these dreams or hallucinations or whatever they were merely defense mechanisms designed to distract me from offing myself, or something more? I'd spent the rest of the afternoon wracking my brain for any clue or tidbit of understanding, but came up empty.

Sophie Dupree blew through the swinging doors into the back, negotiating the sinks and counter area until she'd reached my workspace. "Hey, you taking a break or working straight through?"

"I can take five," I said.

"Cool. I'm gonna go smoke a butt, want to come with?"

I wiped my face and hands with a towel, then undid my apron and tossed it on the counter. "Slowing down any out there?"

"The worst of it's over. Night schedule of movies are starting soon, the bars should start filling up and there's a concert at the bandstand."

"Anybody good playing?"

"Is there ever anybody good playing?"

"Fair enough."

"Might get a few stragglers but should be mostly dead from here on out. Next rush won't be until the breakfast crowd, and we'll be long gone by then."

Nearby, in the kitchen, Demetrius screamed something unintelligible, presumably at one of the other waitresses, and rang the counter bell, signaling an order was ready.

Sophie rolled her eyes, then headed for the diner's heavy steel back door. "Coming?"

I followed her out into a narrow alley.

The night was hot and muggy, but the occasional breeze from the Atlantic felt good. Traffic and walkers on the drag were thinning out. In the distance, I could hear the sounds of a third-rate group rocking out at the bandstand.

As always, I found myself searching for something to say to Sophie. I usually kept to myself, but had no trouble communicating with people if I needed to. For some reason when I got around Sophie I wanted to talk with her but always felt uncertain and awkward.

"That dinner rush was a bitch, huh?" She found a section of wall and leaned back against it, one foot up and pressed flat against it, the other planted firmly on the pavement. She took her cigarettes and a small disposable lighter from her apron and looked up at the moon hanging over the bay. "Another night in paradise," she sighed. "Couple hours and I'll be home with Balthazar, soaking in a cool bathtub, a nice glass of wine at my side and a fatty to go with it. Life is good. Say it with me."

Not long after I'd met Sophie I'd come to learn that Balthazar was her cat. Like me, Sophie was in her middle forties. Divorced, with two grown children, her oldest, a twenty-eight-year-old son, was the result of a teenage romance she'd had at just seventeen, and the other, a daughter and the only child she'd had with her ex-husband, had recently turned twenty-two. All I knew about her son was that he was a mechanic, lived in the western part of the state and was married with children of his own. Her daughter, an aspiring actress, had moved to Los Angeles at eighteen. Far as I could tell, Sophie didn't see her kids or grandkids much, and it obviously bothered her. Like me, I could see in her eyes, in her face, in the way she moved and carried herself, that she knew what it was to be in pain, to be broken.

She knew what it was to be hopeless.

I held up the wall opposite her, folded my arms over my chest and watched the open mouth of the alley to my left.

Sophie hung a cigarette from her lips. "Why do you always do that?"

"Do what?"

"Watch the alley like somebody's about to come around the corner any second?"

I smiled weakly. "Never know."

She flicked the lighter to life and peered at me over the flame with tired eyes. "Something gaining on you, Stan?"

"Something gaining on everybody."

Sophie tilted her head back and blew a stream of smoke up at the black sky. "What's gaining on you?"

I let the night move through me a while. But I never did answer her.

"I've been working in dumps like this and doing this kind of work all my life," she said a moment later. "You're not exactly the type."

"What type am I?"

"Still trying to figure that out." She barely suppressed a smile. "You've got this edge to you that you can't fake. People either have it or they don't. That tells me you've been around the block."

"Yeah?"

"You're too deep to be washing dishes for a living."

"There something wrong with washing dishes for a living?"

"Not at all. Honest work. Hell, I sling food all night, who am I to talk? Just saying you strike me as the type who hasn't always done this kind of thing."

"I could say the same thing about you."

She seemed genuinely flattered. "My depth is all illusion."

"Maybe mine is too."

"You know what I mean. I graduated high school but didn't have the money or grades to go to college. You seem like a deep thinker, a serious guy, I guess, I don't know, maybe I'm not making sense. Wouldn't be the first time." We were quiet a while. Then she said, "I know we don't really know each other that well and it's none of my business, so you can tell me to mind my own if you want, but we've been working together now for what, almost a year, right? I have to ask. How'd you end up here?"

I didn't want to get into it, but she'd never brought it up before, and Sophie was really my only friend at work, so it didn't feel like prying. I got the impression she genuinely wanted to know, and not just out of curiosity, but concern.

"Long time ago," I told her, "I had a different life."

"You're from here originally though, right?" she asked, puffing her cigarette.

"Revere."

"I'm a native Masshole too. My family's from Charlestown original-ly, but we moved up this way when I was in junior high. Been knocking around these parts ever since."

She'd told me that once before but I acted like she hadn't.

"You divorced too?" she asked.

"Yeah."

"Kids?"

Memories I'd managed to avoid for a long time drifted through my mind. "No."

"So I'm right then? You haven't always been a dishwasher extraor-dinaire?"

"Used to be in sales."

"Really? *You?*"

"Wonder of wonders."

"You're not exactly a people person."

I shrugged. "Different time."

Sophie watched me a while, waiting for me to continue.

"Worked sales for a big company out of Boston," I told her. "My wife and I had the whole nine for a while there. Good marriage, nice house, new cars every couple years, vacations—all that—it was like a fairy tale. I had it all there for a second or two."

From her expression alone I could tell Sophie felt sorry for me, but it wasn't in the way I'd come to expect from people. There was nothing demeaning about it. This was compassion, not sympathy.

"Just didn't work out," I said, aware that this was already the most I'd ever said to her in a single conversation. Normally she did the talk-ing and I listened, then responded briefly when it seemed appropriate.

"I'm sorry."

"Don't be. Not all fairy tales have happy endings."

"I thought that was because they don't exist." Sophie smiled but I could tell she realized there was no humor in what I'd said. "You'll have to tell me about it sometime."

"Just did."

"I was thinking maybe more in-depth. Only if you want to, of course."

I nodded but couldn't think of anything more to say.

She drew on her cigarette, exhaled through her nose. A siren blared in the distance, followed by another. "We should go have drinks sometime."

"Okay."

"Yeah?" She smiled, tapped ash.

"Sure." My eyes drifted to the mouth of the alley again. "Why not?"

She blew out another burst of smoke and chuckled softly. "You crack me up."

"Yeah, I'm a regular laugh riot."

"Just comes naturally, huh?"

"It's a gift."

"You're always so serious and kind of...well...don't take this the wrong way but...kind of spooky and detached. It's okay, I mean, I kind of like it if you want to know the truth."

I didn't have a response for her, so I didn't give her one.

Something in her face changed, shifted. "You okay, Stan?"

"Yeah," I sighed.

"Seems like you've got a lot on your mind tonight, more than usual even."

"Bad dreams," I said quietly.

"I'm sorry."

I shrugged, smiled and tried to fake my way through it.

"If you ever need to talk," she said, "I'm around, okay?"

Before I could answer, I was rescued by the sudden uproar of Demetrius screaming and ranting at a member of the staff he'd apparently cornered in the kitchen. His outburst was followed by the sound of a dish smashing.

"Come on," Sophie said, flicking her cigarette into the night. "Let's get back in there before Spartacus has an aneurism."

Two hours later my shift was over. Sophie offered to give me a lift, but I opted to walk instead. I liked to get out into the open air after a shift, helped get some of the stink off and made me feel better. I wandered off into the night and headed for home, which was less than a ten-minute stroll. It was after ten, so things had grown quieter on the strip, the traffic much lighter, but the night people still milled about, the families and touristy types replaced by ghosts moving from one bar to another, walking the beaches or hanging on corners and in the park. The humidity was high as ever, and the earlier ocean breeze had died down, making things even more stagnant, oppressive and sticky, so I decided to stop off at a convenience store for a couple things.

The air-conditioning was a welcome change, so I took my time. As I slowly drifted up one aisle and down another, I tried to get my mind around everything that had happened. Just a few hours prior, I'd been seconds from stepping off this planet for good. Now here I was, sweaty, exhausted, reeking of diner food and browsing the mouthwatering assortment of overpriced frozen dinners.

I selected something with chicken and pasta, then grabbed a can of Coke. A younger, curly-haired, heavyset guy in shorts, flip-flops and a T-shirt emblazoned with the words CAPE COD was drunkenly staggering around the microwave counter fiddling with the wrapper on a burrito of some sort and swearing at it under his breath. I always thought the local T-shirts should've read NOT QUITE CAPE COD as Sunset was about five minutes from the bridges, not on Cape Cod proper, and tended to be the destination of those tourists who couldn't afford a vacation on actual Cape Cod.

"You believe this, brah?" The guy held up his still-wrapped burrito and shook it at me, his eyes bleary but desperate. "It's mystery meat wrapped in a tortilla, not the secrets to the universe. Why is it so hard to open?"

"I got nothing," I mumbled. Brushing by him, I approached the counter, put my things down, then decided to add a couple Slim Jims to the mix.

"Is that it?" a twentysomething cashier with short dark hair and heavy eye makeup asked.

She didn't look familiar, so I figured her for a summer-hire. "Yeah, all set."

After ringing up my order, she gave me the total and I handed her my debit card. She ran it through her machine and a few seconds later it came back declined.

I assured her it was a mistake, so she ran it again. Three tries later, the answer was still the same: DECLINED.

I stood there, more annoyed than embarrassed, trying to understand how this was possible. Bolted to the side of the counter, the credit card machine's small screen blinked my rejection in big bright letters just in case I'd missed it.

"There must be a problem on your end," I said.

The cashier snapped her chewing gum and explained there was nothing else she could do.

"I come in here all the time, use this same card, never have any problems," I said. "Do me a favor and run it one more time, would you?"

With a dramatic sigh, she did. Same result.

"This doesn't make any sense, I have plenty of money in that account."

"Maybe, like, you could try, like, a credit card or something?"

"I don't, *like*, have a credit card. I have a debit card. *This* debit card."

"You can pay cash if you want."

I returned the card to my wallet and rifled through the main compartment, where I located a grand total of seven dollars. I had to put the Slim Jims back but I had enough. "Here," I said, dropping a crumpled five and two ones on the counter.

She threw my dinner and Coke in a plastic bag. I snatched it up and headed for the door. Behind me I heard Burrito Boy say, "Seriously, somebody help me open this or I swear to God I'm going Old Testament on this motherfucker!"

As I stepped back out into the oven of night, I transferred the bag to one hand, then grabbed my cell with the other and dialed my bank. After numerous menus and pressing a series of numbers, I finally reached the 24-hour customer service department and a very chipper representative with a thick Indian accent allegedly named Tabitha. Once I'd provided the answers to a handful of security questions, she checked my bank account.

"Mr. Falk, I show your checking account balance at forty-seven cents."

I stopped at the corner. "That's not possible. I just deposited my paycheck yesterday. We get paid on Wednesdays. I deposit it every Thursday morning on my way to work."

"I'm pulling up a list of your recent deposits," she said cheerily. "Yes, there it is. It posted yesterday morning."

"Then where is it now?"

"According to your recent activity, all but forty-seven cents was withdrawn late last night from an ATM."

"I didn't withdraw any money last night."

"Did you misplace or lose your debit card?"

"Obviously not, I just tried to use it and was denied at the store."

"I understand you have it *now*," Tabitha said in a tone that illustrated my petulance was powerless against her. "I meant could someone else have had access to it last night?"

"No, I've had it the entire time. It's been in my wallet, where it always is."

"And I see you're the only one on the account."

"That's correct."

"I think it's best I deactivate your debit card at this time, Mr. Falk. If you didn't make this withdrawal—"

"How could funds be withdrawn from one of your ATMs without my card?"

"The card is required to access the ATM, sir."

"Then there's a major problem here, because I have the only card and I didn't withdraw any funds last night."

"I understand. What I can do is—"

"Wait, what do *I* do? I need that money."

"I'm freezing the account and deactivating the card so no further transactions can be made. If anyone tries to use the card or card numbers, they will be denied."

"So my last forty-seven cents is safe, thank God."

"Yes, sir."

Apparently Tabitha was unfamiliar with sarcasm. "How do I get a new card?"

"I'm going to issue you one. It should arrive in the mail in approximately seven business days. It is our recommendation that you visit your local branch as soon as possible and speak with the manager so we can assist you in notifying the police and taking the necessary steps to get to the bottom of this."

"Can you tell me which ATM the money was withdrawn from?"

The sound of Tabitha clicking away on her keyboard drifted through the phone. "The Eagle Street branch in Sunset, Massachusetts."

"That's my local branch, the one I always use."

"Our records indicate the withdrawal occurred at 12:36 last night."

I thought for a moment. Last night I'd gotten out of work at eleven like always. I'd hit my usual liquor store on the way home, then...then what? I went home and drank myself to sleep. Didn't I? I'd known then what I had planned for the following morning and I wanted to drink myself into oblivion. Could I have gone back out and withdrawn that money? Didn't seem possible. I'd had blackouts before but not to that extent. And even if I had taken the money out, what the hell did I do with it? Wasn't possible I'd done that, then spent it and forgotten the entire thing. That check was the last thing on my mind. The only reason I'd even bothered to deposit it in the first place was pure spite. I didn't want Demetrius to be able to cancel it and keep it after my death. It was mine. I'd earned every penny of it, why should I let him keep it?

"Wasn't me," I said. "I got out of work at eleven. I was home by then."

"I'm going to email this information to your branch manager and let her know you'll be in to see her."

"There's got to be surveillance footage from the ATM, right?"

"That's something you'd need to discuss with your branch manager, sir."

"Yeah, okay. Thanks."

"You're very welcome, sir. I'm so sorry this happened. Hopefully it's all just a terrible misunderstanding. Good luck."

In my experience, good luck was rarely wished upon those likely to receive it.

I disconnected the call, stepped off the curb and crossed the street, moving along a sidewalk that paralleled the boatyard, wharf and public beach, all of which were quiet and dark, but for a bonfire in the distance. I pictured people gathered around, drinking and eating and laughing. That kind of thing seemed so foreign to me. It had for a very long time.

I kept moving, past the hotel and movie theater and up the steep hill that led to the more residential part of town. The last twenty-four hours could sincerely kiss my ass. I'd nearly killed myself. Horrific nightmares and freakish visions had tormented me. And since that evidently wasn't sufficient, now some asshole had managed to rob me of what little money I had in the first place.

Drifting through the darkness, all I could smell was ocean. Once I'd reached the summit of the hill and was back on relatively level ground, I heard waves gently lapping the shore below. It had become a signal of sorts.

I was home. Such as it was.

Following a path to the bluff, I fumbled keys from my pocket and closed on my cottage, which sat dark and empty in the night.

Until the glow of an orange ember appeared, stopping me in my tracks.

There, in the dark, a black silhouette stood by my front door manically smoking a cigarette.

3

FROM THE SHADOWS, A face emerged—thankfully not my own—filthy, covered in stubble and bathed in the glow of the cigarette. "Hey, Stan."

Apprehension dissolved into relief. "Duane, what are you doing out here?"

A local homeless man I'd befriended a few months before, Duane smoked his cigarettes with feverish repetition, one drag after another until they burned to the filters, then he'd normally light another from the butt of the last. "Just waiting on you to come home." He motioned casually to the light next to my front door. "You should leave the outside light on when you leave so you can see better."

"Yeah," I said, moving by him.

"You have a good night at work?" he asked.

"Spectacular." I unlocked the door, reached inside and flipped the outside light on. Often as I could, I brought him something to eat from the diner, but he knew I couldn't swing it every night. "Sorry, couldn't get you anything this time."

"No problem," he said, running a free hand through his thick, unwashed hair.

Duane was younger than me but looked at least ten years older.

"Money's tight," I told him. "And Demetrius is a prick about donating food."

"Sure, Stan. No biggie."

"You know how it is."

"Ain't like it's your responsibility, dude."

It occurred to me I hadn't seen Duane in a few days. The cops left him alone in the fall and winter months, but in summer, with all the tourists, having homeless guys wandering the streets wasn't exactly good for business, so they hassled him a lot. It wasn't unusual for him to disappear for days at a clip, but he'd eventually always find his way back to my door. "How long since you had something to eat?"

He straightened the near-rags he called clothes. Despite the heat, he always wore multiple shirts and sometimes even a jacket or heavy coat. As a result, he was always slick with perspiration. "Had me some Chinese takeout night before last."

That was code for he'd raided the local Chinese restaurant's Dumpster after hours. I glanced down at the bag in my hand. "Tell you what. Give me a minute to change and wash up and I'll split a frozen dinner with you."

"You don't have to do that."

"Yeah, I know. I'll split it with you anyway, cool?"

"Most cool." He flashed his brown-toothed smile, sat on the bench to the right of the door and pulled a small bottle of cheap whiskey from his pocket. "Got the beverage covered, Poncho let me sweep up over at the arcade, paid me with a couple pints. Already killed one but still got number two."

"It's okay, hang on to it. I've got some beers in the fridge. I'll grab you one."

Duane nodded, his dark, bloodshot eyes heavy with perpetual sorrow. "Thanks, man."

"Be right out."

"Take your time. I got nothing but."

It felt strange in the cottage now, in light of what I'd almost done. I closed the door behind me and stood there a moment until my nerves settled. This was still home, the only one I had.

I dropped everything on the kitchen table, threw the frozen dinner in the microwave, then headed into the bathroom. After changing into a pair of shorts and a tank top, I threw some cool water on my face, then ran some through my hair.

By the time I'd snatched a couple cans of beer from the fridge and torn us each a piece of paper towel for napkins, the microwave sounded. I pulled the plastic tray out and peeled away the plastic covering it. It didn't smell half-bad but looked like someone had already chewed it for us. There was barely enough there to feed a young child, but I emptied half of it onto a paper plate, grabbed a couple forks, then joined Duane outside on the bench.

"Smells good," he said, carefully butting his cigarette on the ground, then pocketing it before rubbing his hands together in eager anticipation. "What we got?"

"I don't know, some sort of chicken with pasta in what I think is supposed to be Alfredo sauce." I handed him the paper plate, a fork and a beer. "Bon appétit."

Holding the plate with one hand, Duane shoveled the food in with the other, chewing noisily. "God*damn*, that's pretty good!"

I picked at mine with a fork, stabbed a small piece of chicken and a bow tie and gave it a try. "Duane, it tastes like ass."

"*Delicious* ass," he said, jamming another mouthful in.

Once he'd finished his, I handed him the rest of mine.

"You sure?"

"Trust me, I'm sure."

Duane pounced on it and the shoveling commenced. "Thanks, man, you're the best!"

I sipped some beer. It was ice-cold and felt good going down.

He grabbed his can and held it up so I could tap it with mine. Once I had, he took a long pull, let out a thunderous belch, then quickly finished up the rest of his dinner. "That was badass," he said, retrieving his cigarette butt from his pocket. "Thanks, Stan."

"What did I tell you about that? You don't have to keep thanking me, all right? I do it because I want to."

"What can I say?" He fired up his disposable lighter with filthy hands and took a hard drag on what remained of his cigarette. "My parents taught me right. Somebody does you a solid, you say thank you."

I often found myself wondering how Duane had wound up homeless and living on the streets. But then I realized most were just a paycheck or two away from it. Couple bad moves or an unexpected tragedy and who knew where any of us might be. Truth was, it was a minor miracle I'd avoided a similar fate and hadn't somehow descended to such depths myself. We'd never discussed how he'd come to be in his present condition, and I had no plans to ask. If Duane wanted me to know, he'd tell me.

"You haven't seen anything weird around town lately, have you?" I asked.

"Maybe you didn't notice. Everybody and everything around here's weird."

"That's not what I mean."

"Ain't seen nothing out of the ordinary." Duane straightened his posture. "Why, you having trouble? Somebody giving you some trouble, Stan?"

"No, nothing like that."

"You sure? 'Cause if you're having trouble, I got your back, man."

"I appreciate it, but I'm fine."

We were quiet a while.

"I'm just glad you're not mad at me no more," Duane said.

"Why would I be mad at you?"

"Well, you know." He fidgeted about uneasily. "After last night and all."

"Last night?"

"Figured you were mad since you didn't say nothing."

"Duane, what the hell are you talking about?"

"Sorry, I…" He scratched at the back of his head and squinted his eyes as if he were trying his best to remember. "You know I get confused sometimes. It was last night, wasn't it? Yeah, it was. Last night, remember? I saw you downtown and I said hi and you walked right by me so I figured you had a bad day or maybe you were just mad at me for something. I know I—I can be a pain in the ass sometimes."

"Are you drunk?"

"Of course." Duane looked at me as if I'd lost my mind. "I'm always fucking drunk. That's kind of my thing, being a drunk."

"You're confused," I told him. "I haven't seen you in a few days."

He nervously scratched at his neck, then gulped some beer. "Okay, Stan."

I'd tied on a good one but had I left the house I would've remembered. "What time was this, when you thought you saw me?"

"Almost one," he said. "I know 'cause the big electronic sign outside the hardware store said 12:50. You were walking down the drag and I was across the street having a drink and grooving on the moon, sitting on the bench over by the hot dog stand. I called out to you and said hey and you looked right at me but kept walking. You didn't wave or say hi or nothing, so I figured you were pissed at me."

"Wasn't me, Duane."

He nodded, though I could tell he was only placating me. "Okay."

I could only hope my sudden apprehension wasn't evident. "Must've been someone that looked like me," I told him.

Duane stood up, sending the pungent smell of body odor and rancid bad breath wafting all around us. Oblivious, he killed his beer and placed the empty on the bench next to me. "Getting late, I better get down to the sand before the cops start cruising the streets. They been giving me a lot of shit lately, you know how they are once the tourists show up."

"All right, man," I said, ignoring memories of my mangled face. "Be safe."

He dug a wrinkled pack of cigarettes from his pocket, stabbed one in his mouth and lighted it. "Damn," he mumbled, "almost out of smokes."

As he headed for the rear of the cottage and the path that led down to the dunes and beach below, I stood up and stretched a bit. The night was getting sticky and more oppressive, the rare ocean breeze no longer helping much. "Hey, Duane?"

He stopped, looked back at me.

"You sure it was me you saw?"

"Nah," he said softly. "It was late and I was drinking all day so I was out of it. Besides, you said it wasn't you, right?"

I shook my head no.

"Then like you said, must've been somebody that looked like you."

Voices from the beach below—likely those of a couple walking along the waterline—echoed along the dunes, up the bluff, then drifted away, carried off on a gentle night wind.

Duane vanished around the side of the cottage, leaving me with my confusion and a mounting uneasiness. What the hell was going on? Terrifying dreams, strange hallucinations, my bank account mysteriously emptied, and now Duane claiming to have seen me on the street when I knew damn well I was in bed and passed out from a night of hard drinking. None of it made a bit of sense.

Despite the heat, an icy vulnerability seized hold of me, as if the ordinary, the *usual*, no longer existed.

Gathering our trash from the bench, I slipped back inside.

From the back of my mind, the distant echo of screams followed close behind.

39

4

FROM MY POSITION ON *the floor, on my side in the fetal position, the mirror on the wall is too high for me to gaze into. But I can see shadows sweeping across it, gliding phantoms there, then gone. Like the woman…gone. They took her.*

I don't want to move because I don't want to disturb the bones. They make a horrible sound when they're disturbed, and the noise awakens and agitates the spiders.

Blinking until my vision focuses, my eyes are drawn to the ceiling. The spiders have gone quiet, just like everything else. Nothing moves. Nothing makes a sound. Not even me. Especially me.

It smells like death here, like dead and decayed things have resided here for a very long time. And yet, there is fresh death here as well. There is blood among the bones, smeared on the walls, drawn into symbols and words, an ancient language I don't understand.

I look away from the spiders. I don't—I can't—look at them anymore. I want to get up and run away from here but I can't get up. There's something wrong with me, something not right. Something's controlling me, keeping me on this hideous floor of bloody bones despite my best efforts to escape it.

On the wall, a crude painting of an old man lords over me. Even in the limited light, I see he is sitting on a throne of sorts. His hair is long and unruly, as is his beard. In his hand he holds a scythe, and he is surrounded by numerous symbols written in blood that look similar to the letter T.

"Come," a male voice says from the shadows. "Come and see."

Somewhere in the distance, from some other dark corner of this old abandoned building, I hear screams...horrible screams of unimaginable agony.

The woman. They're killing her.

And I'm next.

* * *

I came awake with a thunderous headache, bathed in sweat and out of breath. I was alone, and the ceiling above me was the same old cracked and stained plaster it had always been. Despite the multiple fans I had going, the humidity was already unbearable. Another scorcher of a day lay ahead.

Two cups of coffee, a handful of aspirin and a long, cool shower later, I felt better and finally beyond the grasp of the nightmare that had torn me from sleep.

My bank was only open until noon on Saturdays, so I called and spoke briefly with the branch manager, a pleasant woman named Ginny-Anne. She told me she'd received the information regarding my "account dispute" and was aware of my concerns, so I explained I'd be in to see her shortly. Since my bank wasn't far, I decided to walk rather than drive.

Sunset was slowly coming to life, the morning air thick with the smell of fried breakfast foods. In the distance, the gleeful yelps and screeches of children signaled the waterpark a few blocks over was already hopping. I found the veracity of that sound at once unpleasant and alluring, as it possessed a shameless abandon I both envied and resented. It also reminded me of things I only wanted to forget.

Once I'd reached the plaza where my bank was located, I entered the lobby through the ATM area, told one of the tellers I needed to see the manager, then waited for her in a comfortable chair just outside her office. The air-conditioning was cranked to the point that by the time Ginny-Anne emerged from behind her closed door to greet me, I was freezing. But it was preferable to the stifling heat, so I went with it, rising and shaking her hand as I introduced myself.

An attractive heavyset woman in her forties, she flashed a brilliant white smile and did her best to be accommodating and pleasant, but the moment she got a good look at me, something changed in her expression. It was a subtle change but unmistakable. "Mr. Falk," she said in a squeaky, childlike voice that didn't match her appearance, "it's a pleasure to meet you. I'm sorry it's under these circumstances."

"Thanks for seeing me."

I followed her into her office. She motioned to a chair in front of her desk. "Please, have a seat." Rather than sit in her leather swivel, she sat on the edge of her desk. "I understand there's some confusion regarding your account and a recent ATM withdrawal, is that correct?"

"There's no confusion. I didn't make the withdrawal."

"So you're disputing the ATM withdrawal this past Thursday evening?"

"Yes."

She smiled again. "I just wanted to be sure I understood you correctly."

"I deposited my paycheck Thursday morning, like I do every week."

"Yes, I reviewed our records and that deposit posted to your account."

"Right, but your records also indicate I made an ATM withdrawal that night."

"Technically Friday morning, since it was after midnight, but yes, that's correct," she said with an efficient nod. "Leaving you with a current balance of forty-seven cents."

I forced a smile of my own. "Problem is, I never went to the ATM Thursday night and never made any withdrawals, so there's got to be some mistake."

Ginny-Anne's smile faded. "Is it possible, Mr. Falk, that you simply forgot you made the withdrawal, or did so accidentally?"

"No," I sighed, my patience already waning, "it's not."

"As I'm sure you're well aware, all our ATM locations are outfitted with surveillance cameras." She turned her computer monitor around so I could see the screen, then leaned back across her desk and tapped her keyboard. "Once I received the information regarding your dispute, I located the footage that corresponded with the time code for the withdrawal."

A new window popped up onto the monitor, showing a perfect view of the ATM area and even the entrance to the bank. "If you notice the stamp on the bottom right of the screen," she said, pointing to it with a long fingernail painted a shade of bright blue that matched the color of her skirt-suit. "It clearly displays the day, date and time."

I sat forward so I could get a closer look. The footage was black-and-white but crystal clear. "Okay."

"This past Friday at 12:36 a.m., see?"

Before I could agree again, a man suddenly appeared at the glass door. It opened and the man stepped inside, moved to the ATM and looked directly into the camera.

For a moment I had no idea what I was looking at, because it simply wouldn't register, much less compute. My heart raced, I felt a tightening in my gut and, despite the chill in the office, a rush of heat surged through me, leaving me stunned and light-headed. "I don't...I don't understand," I heard myself say, my voice foreign and detached, like it belonged to someone else.

I was looking at myself. Again. There was no question, and this time my face was fine, undamaged. I was the man in the video. I watched as I withdrew a stack of bills, then turned and left.

"Wouldn't you agree that's obviously you, Mr. Falk?"

I nodded, my mouth open. "I—can I see that again, please?"

"Certainly."

She tapped her keys and the tape played again. This time I looked at my eyes. They seemed off. I looked distracted. Calm and completely in control of myself, but distracted. I was wearing the same clothes I'd worn to work that day, a pair of jeans and a sleeveless T-shirt, the red and white bandana I often wore during my shift still tied to my head. "I don't understand," I mumbled.

"It's an honest mistake."

I sat back, baffled and more than a little frightened. A hallucination—a nightmare—however horrific, was one thing. This was something else entirely. This was real. "I have no memory of making that withdrawal."

Ginny-Anne turned her monitor back to its proper position, then slid off the edge of her desk, walked around behind it and sank down into her leather swivel. "People often forget transactions, Mr. Falk," she said sweetly. "They confuse or mix up days and times, happens all the time."

"I don't see how this is possible, I—"

"It really isn't that unusual, believe me."

How the hell could I have withdrawn that money and have no memory of it? And what did I do with it? None of this made any sense. It wasn't me. It *couldn't* be me. But it was. I'd seen the tape with my own eyes. Twice.

"I'm sorry, I—"

"Don't be. As I say, these things happen. Simple misunderstanding." Ginny-Anne retrieved a sheet of paper from her desk drawer and held it out to me. "In the video you don't appear to take your receipt, so I've taken the liberty of printing you a copy for your records."

Suddenly all I wanted was to get out of there. I stood up, took the receipt and turned for the door. "I apologize for the confusion," I said without looking back. "Thanks, I—I'm sorry for wasting your time, I—"

"You did no such thing, sir. I'm just happy we were able to clear this up."

I staggered out of the bank and into the heat. The world was spinning, my mind struggling to get around what I'd just seen as I teetered on the brink of absolute panic. I needed to get off the street, and fast. I needed to go somewhere quiet and think, to sort this all out and try to make some sense of a situation that, by its very nature, belied logic. I needed a drink.

The drag was filling up with tourists, and everything was louder and more congested now. I walked quickly, head down, until I reached my cottage.

Inside, I grabbed a glass and what was left of a bottle of Jack Daniel's from the cupboard, and while standing at the sink, poured myself a shot and powered it down. I quickly did another, and then a third. My hands finally stopped shaking.

I paced about the kitchen. Could it be possible I'd gotten so wasted the other night that I completely forgot I'd gone to the ATM? Had I taken that money out, then blown it somewhere, at one of the local watering holes maybe? If so, someone would've seen me, someone could verify this.

Duane. He saw me walking home that night. At 12:50, fourteen minutes after I'd withdrawn the money. So where was I from 11:00 to 12:36? I could cover the ground between home and the bank in about five minutes, so if after the ATM I'd walked directly back to my cottage, it shouldn't have taken anywhere near fourteen minutes to do so. Had I moved at a slower pace purposely or without realizing it? Even if I had, there remained more than an hour and a half unaccounted for.

Did I even remember getting home that night? No.

"Okay," I said aloud. "Wait. Think."

What *did* I recall about Thursday night? I walked myself through it.

I remembered Thursday as a particularly busy shift. I was exhausted and left work at the usual time. After that, things got hazy. Until then, I'd chalked it up to having gotten so drunk that night, but now that I was attempting to piece together the day as a whole, I was coming up short. I vaguely remembered drinking and stumbling around the cottage later that evening and eventually collapsing into bed, but I had no idea of the actual times.

On a regular shift, which is what I'd worked Thursday, I was out at 11:00. Where was I from 11:00 to 12:36?

"Christ," I muttered, putting the bottle and glass aside.

I was missing a grand total of an hour and fifty minutes. Nearly two hours. Unless I'd wandered aimlessly around town with no memory of having done so whatsoever, there'd likely be some sort of paper trail. I must've gone somewhere.

I hurried into my bedroom and dug through the hamper until I found the jeans I'd worn on Thursday. I searched the pockets, came up with my paycheck stub, half a pack of Juicy Fruit I remembered buying the weekend before, and at first glance what appeared to be a black business card. No receipts, no cash. Not even any loose change.

I tossed the check stub and gum on my bureau, draped the jeans over my arm and took a closer look at the business card. It was completely black. No letters or numbers, graphics or other information. Nothing indicating what it was, just a blank black business card. What was I doing with it in the first place? Had someone given it to me? If so, why? Who printed a completely blank black business card? I had no knowledge or memory of what it was or how I'd come to possess it.

But I did *feel* something. Something strange. From the moment I held it in my hand, I became even more nervous and uncomfortable. Unsettled. At the very outskirts of my memory, odd blurs and flashes twisted past my mind's eye, but I couldn't make any sense of them. It was like coming awake from a nightmare and being unable to remember anything other than the fact that I had dreamed. All else remained just beyond reach.

I threw the jeans back into the hamper and, card still in hand, returned to the kitchen, pulled out a chair and sat at the table. Something had happened to me. I'd been depressed to the point that I'd planned to commit suicide. Did I snap or have a breakdown I was unaware of? Could I have gone into a trance or something, some odd state that caused those hallucinations of a double, riddled me with nightmares and left me with no memory of where I'd been or what I'd done? Was that kind of thing even possible? And what the hell was I supposed to do for money until next week? That cash was all I had. There was no savings account, no retirement fund or backup money for me to dip into. I washed dishes for a living.

Placing the card on the table before me, I did my best to concentrate.

I couldn't remember a damn thing.

Maybe the razor wasn't such a bad alternative after all. Maybe I should've gone through with it like I'd planned. Maybe I needed to stop delaying the inevitable and just do it. Maybe—

My phone began to ring, startling me. The old man again.

He obviously wasn't going to leave me alone until I went to see what he wanted, so without bothering to answer the call, I slid the business card—or whatever it was—into my wallet and headed out the door.

5

A LITTLE OVER AN hour later, I passed through Boston and into Revere. Named after Paul Revere, the city was home to the Necco candy company, Kelly's Roast Beef, the birthplace of the modern roast beef sandwich, and the old Wonderland Greyhound Park. The hometown to Red Sox great "Tony C," Tony Conigliaro, and movie star John Cazale, like anywhere else, there was good and bad here. There were some very nice sections of the city, but the neighborhood I'd grown up in near the beach wasn't one of them. My old stomping grounds hadn't changed much and probably never would. Growing up in a tough neighborhood, I became accustomed to physical confrontation from the time I was a kid. It had been years since I'd strong-armed or been strong-armed by anyone, but that sort of thing was never far. Violence was like that. It was like an addiction, always there, just waiting for that moment of weakness, that opening that might allow it back. Because it never really left you, no matter how long you turned your back on it. Sooner or later, it knew damn well you'd look its way, and when you did, it'd be ready.

The street I grew up on was lined with modest duplexes and old three-story homes long ago converted into apartments, most of the tiny yards surrounded by chain-link fence. I hadn't been back in months, but every time I returned I was flooded with bad memories I'd spent a lifetime trying to forget.

While I had some good memories here as well, few of them meant anything to me anymore. My mother was long dead, I had no brothers or sisters, and my father was an asshole with whom I had virtually no relationship. The house I'd grown up in represented nothing to me but money. When the bastard eventually kicked, it'd go to me, and I planned to sell it fast as I could, then take the money and run. Once he and the house were gone, I'd never have to come back here again.

I parked a ways down the street in the first spot I could find, then walked back to the house. Just like in Sunset, it was hot here but the smell and sounds of the ocean were always close. Somewhere along the block a dog barked incessantly, a siren howled in the distance and I stood before the screen door on the old and slowly rotting steps of the house I lived in for the first nineteen years of my life. The main door was open, but because of the sunlight I couldn't see into the house. I could hear a television though, and the smell of food that had gone bad wafted out through the screen. While trying to convince myself to go inside, I noticed the little things I usually missed. The house was in serious need of a paint job. The gate to the patch of front yard was rusted so badly it needed to be replaced. The grass was at least knee-high and likely hadn't been mowed all season, and the curtains that hung in the windows were filthy and mostly in tatters. How many times had I sat on these steps as a child, covering my ears and trying hard as I could to block out the sounds coming from inside the house? How many times had I dreamed of other places, other people, other lives?

The screen door was unlocked, so I yanked it open and stepped into the past.

I hadn't been there in six months or more, and while the place was always a mess, things had gotten far worse since my last visit. The house hadn't been cleaned or even straightened up in a very long time, and it not only looked like it, it smelled like it.

My eyes drifted to the staircase before me. Visions of my father dragging my mother by her hair down those same stairs flashed in my head. I could so vividly remember the sound the back of her head made as it slapped each step it was as if it were still happening all these years later, interspersed with my own boyish cries as I begged him to stop.

"Who's there?" my father called from the den, his voice slurred. "I got a gun, fuck-nut!"

"Relax, Pop," I called, walking past the staircase and along the narrow hallway that led to the den and, eventually, the kitchen. "It's just me."

I found him collapsed in a battered recliner in the den, watching a Red Sox game on an old tube television sitting atop a cart in the corner. In a soiled tank top and a pair of shorts, he was barefoot and looked like he hadn't bathed in some time. It had also been a while since he'd shaved, as his face was covered in a good amount of gray stubble. Bald on top, he had a horseshoe of white hair around the sides of his head that was in serious need of a trim and thorough shampooing. An old folding table stood next to the recliner, a half-eaten bowl of Spaghetti-Os and a plastic ashtray brimming with cigar butts and ash strewn across it. Numerous empty beer cans cluttered the floor, along with several spent bottles of vodka.

"What did you do, bust the door?"

"It was unlocked," I told him. "You need to be careful about that."

He looked up and squinted, like he couldn't quite see me. "I've been waiting on you. What the hell took you so long?"

"I had shit to do," I said, looking around. "Jesus, Pop, don't you have Mrs. Torres come in and clean anymore?"

"Fired her fat spic ass."

"Why would you do that? Look at this place."

"It don't matter." He waved at the air between us, grabbed the TV remote from his lap and lowered the volume on the baseball game. "Fucking Sox, pissing me off for a change."

"It matters," I told him. "The place is a mess. And it smells."

"Who gives a shit?" He tossed the remote onto the table and belched loudly. "Go get us a couple beers out of the fridge, I need to talk to you."

"I'm good."

"Well, I'm not, I'm thirsty. Go get me one, you rude bastard."

With a sigh I returned to the hallway and followed it down to the kitchen, doing my best to ignore the photographs on the walls he insisted on keeping up. I couldn't stand to look at them. There was nothing real about them, nothing genuine, just a bunch of people pretending and smiling for the camera.

The kitchen was in worse shape than the rest of the house. Flies buzzed everywhere and roaches crawled across a mountain of dishes in the sink. The stench was nearly unbearable, and from the condition of the wall behind the stove, it was obvious there had been a small fire here not long ago. I opened the refrigerator, found a half gallon of soured milk, some leftover slices of pizza thrown on a paper plate and haphazardly covered in plastic wrap, and a case of beer.

I pulled a can free of the plastic rings and returned to the den, ignoring one memory in particular, when my father, in a drunken rage, had pinned me to that kitchen floor and pummeled me until I was unconscious. I was nine at the time.

"You have a fire?" I asked as I handed him the beer.

"Yeah, no big whoop." He popped the tab, took several gulps, then nodded. "Forgot I had something going on the stove. Burned the wall a little is all, fire department didn't even need to come."

I'd always known that if my father lived long enough, there would come a time when he'd have to go into a nursing home or assisted living situation. Apparently, that time had arrived.

"It's none of your concern anyway, boy." He pointed to a chair in the corner covered in old newspapers and junk mail. "And like I said, none of it matters, so sit down and shut up and let me tell you what's going on."

I sat on the edge of the chair without bothering to push the trash onto the floor.

"You remember my buddy Joey Strizziano? Him and Lucille moved down to Florida last year. They got this place where they take care of you and shit, it's like a village but you still got freedom and you still got your own little place, you see what I'm saying?"

"Assisted living," I said.

"Yeah." He powered down more beer. "Anyways, I'm going down there too."

"How you going to afford that, Pop?"

"I sold the house."

"You sold the house? This house?"

"No, the one down the street, jackass, of course this house. The little real estate slut called me the day before yesterday and told me it sold."

I was stunned. I'd always expected him to either die in this house or leave it to me. It was my only inheritance. I wanted nothing from him, but this had been my mother's house too, and she would've wanted me to have it.

"How the hell did you sell it in this kind of shape?"

"Could've got more if I fixed it up, but I don't have the money for that." He burped again, then wiped his mouth with the back of his hand. "Anyways, I figured I better let you know. I'm leaving for Florida in a couple weeks. Sorry about not being able to leave you the old homestead, boy, but that's how it goes."

"It's your house," I said. "Do whatever you want with it."

"I'd throw you a couple bucks but I need every dime to get me into the place down south."

"Don't worry about it."

He killed his beer, tossed the can on the floor. "I'm not."

"So what do you want from me?" I asked.

"Nothing. I just wanted to let you know."

"You could've told me this over the phone."

He smiled with his bleary eyes. "I wanted to see your face when I told you."

Once a sadist, always a sadist.

"Hope you enjoyed yourself," I said, standing.

He laughed. "Think I came a little."

"I got to go."

"You want anything, you better take it now," he said. "I talked to this guy who can clean the whole place out and take everything to the dump. Mrs. Sims hired him to clean out her garage and he did good by her so I got him coming tomorrow."

Anything to do with this house I'd taken with me long ago, good and bad.

"I'm all set," I told him.

He fidgeted about in the recliner. "So, I—well—I probably won't be seeing you again, boy. Not getting any younger, and all my money's going into this place so I won't be able to afford to travel, you see what I'm saying?"

I nodded.

"When I kick, they'll fly me up here and bury me next to your mother," he said, scratching at his enormous belly. "Until then, you know, maybe swing by and see her grave, make sure those pricks over there are doing the upkeep they're supposed to and all that. And make sure you go by before you leave today and pay your respects, you hear me?"

"I don't go to graveyards."

"You do what I tell you!"

"Mom's not there, Pop."

"Says who?" He stabbed a fat sausage finger at me. "Go pay your respects to your mother like I said!"

"What the hell would you know about respecting my mother?"

He stared at me for several seconds like he couldn't quite comprehend what I'd said. "What the hell you just say to me?"

"You heard me."

He shook his head. "Hell of a way to say goodbye to your old man."

Back when he still could, he would've bloodied me up for talking to him like that. But we both knew those days were long over. "There anything else?"

"Yeah," he said. "You talk to Linda lately?"

I glared at him.

"I'm serious."

"Not in years," I finally answered. "You know that."

"Not for nothing, but I heard she's doing real good now." He smiled.

He knew all the ways to hurt me, and got off on grinding me to dust with every one of them. "Linda was a long time ago, Pop, I'm not talking about this."

"She's a Fancy Nancy these days, you know." He reached down beside the recliner and came back with a bottle of vodka. "Her and her big-shot husband live over in Brookline. Fucking excuse me, right? They got three kids too. She had the hottest little ass I ever seen, and cute tits too, but she wasn't worth your life, boy."

I'd never understood my father, or why he loved to inflict pain on me the way he did. And while it was a horrible thing to stand just feet from the man that helped create me and feel absolutely nothing but contempt for him, I understood all too well why I hated him. I'd just never figured out why he hated me.

"Why are you doing this?"

He swigged from the bottle. "What am I doing?"

"Fucking with me for no reason."

"Because it's so goddamn easy," he chuckled. "Always was."

"Proud of yourself?"

"Whatever," he said, waving me away again. "Just like your mother, neither one of you ever had a sense of humor."

"Little hard to laugh when your lips are split, your eyes are swollen shut and your teeth are in your hands."

"Here we go with this bullshit." He took another long pull from the bottle.

"Oh, I know it. You were a model father and husband, weren't you?"

"I did fine by you and your mother. Food on the table, clothes on your back, roof over your heads. I tried to make you a man, boy, did my best. You just didn't have the juice, kid, you were weak, weren't willing to do the things a man's got to do to be a man."

"What the hell would you know about it?"

"I know this much. You could've been somebody around here, somebody in the neighborhood, but you threw it all away on that little piece of ass."

"I was in love with Linda."

"Yeah," he laughed, "I was *in love* with her too."

"I don't think trying to feel up your daughter-in-law every time you have too much to drink qualifies."

"No?" He laughed. "You sure? Maybe it was just lust then. If you had a brain in your fucking head, it would've been nothing but that for you too. Throw her a good one and get on with shit. But no, you marry the bitch. How'd that work out for you, moron? Think about that every time you wash a dish for minimum wage, you fucking idiot."

There were a million things I wanted to tell him, a million reasons why I wanted to beat him to a pulp like he'd beaten my mother and me dozens of times over the years. But he wasn't worth any of that. He never had been.

"Couldn't even give me a grandkid," he mumbled. "Couldn't even do that right."

"Shut your mouth." I felt my hands tighten into fists. "Shut your filthy fucking mouth."

"I ain't afraid of you."

"You should be, old man."

He had another swallow of vodka but most of it dribbled down his chin and across his chest and belly. He was so drunk he was barely conscious. "Fuck off," he slurred, making a half-assed attempt to throw the bottle at me. It landed a few feet from me and rolled away, spilling whatever was left inside across the floor.

Feeling alone was nothing new for me. I'd been out on a ledge by myself for quite some time. But now I was glad I hadn't stepped off as I'd planned, because for the first time in my life, I also felt truly free of the disease that was my father.

"Good luck in Florida, Pop. Once you get settled in and have your new phone and address, do me a favor, huh?" Without fear, I looked right at him, this pathetic old man who'd frightened me as a child so intensely he could make me pee myself just by raising his voice. "Stick them up your ass. Good and deep, you piece of shit."

"Help me up," he said, dangling a hand out toward me. "I got to take a dump."

Instead, I stood there and let him soil himself.

He was still trying to get out of the recliner, sloshing around in his own mess and muttering obscenities at me when I left.

Glad to be back out on the steps, away from him and his stench, I stood there and let the sun wash over me. It felt good. Almost as good as knowing that I'd never set foot anywhere near here again.

For just a few minutes, I forgot about straight razors and the life I'd almost thrown away, the times I'd spent on these mean streets, the happiness I'd once had, then let slip through my fingers, grimy diners and endless piles of dishes, strange visions at my door, lost time, empty bank accounts and creepy blank business cards.

For a while, all those storms went quiet, but unlike me, I knew they'd be back sooner or later. I hurried to my car and headed for the cape, as if to hold a lead on them, realizing then that this place was no longer home for me, hadn't been in a very long time.

And for that, I could only be grateful.

6

THE DRIVE BACK WAS long and strange, my head filled with old memories and new nightmares, both fighting for purchase in my already exhausted mind. Nothing seemed right or real, the road, the car, the skies, all of it like some giant canopy spread out and prepared to distract me from the things nesting beneath.

I wanted nothing more than to drink myself into oblivion and sleep away the rest of this day, this life, but as I pulled into the spot alongside my cottage, I noticed my neighbor and landlord Albert Smithee sweeping his small porch. The cottages were all relatively close to each other in our neighborhood, the plots quite modest, but Albert, who owned his place and mine, had one of the nicer and larger cottages on our road, complete with a carport, a spacious deck and Jacuzzi out back and a small porch in front. Although well into his sixties, Albert looked much younger and was in terrific shape from years of yoga and tai chi, both of which he practiced with great discipline on his deck overlooking the Atlantic. Originally from Pennsylvania, he'd owned and operated a real estate agency that was so successful he was able to sell it and retire while still in his fifties. He and his longtime girlfriend Carla, a high school history teacher, spent their summers in Sunset and the remainder of the year in their town house in Philadelphia. Because the three of us had always gotten along well, and likely because they felt sorry for me, they allowed me to pay much less than the going rate in exchange for looking after both cottages in the winter months. Were it not for their kindness, I would've never been able to afford the rent.

Albert waved to me. "Hey, Stan," he called, "got a sec?"

Climbing out of my run-down Chevy, I waved back, moved across the front of my cottage and over to the steps of his porch. "Sure," I said listlessly. "What's up?"

"Is everything all right?"

I wasn't exactly sure how to answer that so I simply said, "Yeah. Why?"

"Just wondering what yesterday was about."

"Yesterday?"

Albert's lean, sinewy frame, clad only in a pair of gray cotton shorts, was tanned a deep brown, as it was every summer. "You don't remember?" he asked.

"I'm sorry, I—remember what?"

"I happened to be up yesterday morning," he said. A notorious night owl, Albert normally didn't get up until early afternoon. "I couldn't sleep, so I decided to go for a run on the beach. I was on my way back when I saw you at your door. I thought maybe you'd locked yourself out or something."

Despite the heat, I suddenly felt cold. Had Albert seen the same thing I had? Was there really someone knocking at my door yesterday, stopping me from running that razor across my wrists, someone that looked like me, his face savaged?

Stunned, I stood there staring at him. "I'm sorry, Albert. I didn't see you."

"Well, that's the thing. You did."

"I did?" I asked helplessly, trying to mask my confusion with light laughter.

Albert stopped sweeping, leaned on his broom and ran a hand over his closely cropped salt-and-pepper hair. "Are you serious?"

"Yes."

"I looked right at you and asked what was wrong," Albert explained. "You were behaving very strangely—jittery and nervous—almost as if you weren't sure where you were, and you had a hoodie on with the hood up. I asked if you were all right and you mumbled something and stood staring at your door. You didn't go inside. I tried to engage you in conversation and you completely ignored me. I was really worried about you."

My heart crashed my chest. "Sorry, man, I had too much to drink."

"At that hour? Look, I'm all for having a good time, and God knows I'll party with the best of them when it's the right place and time, but this was—Stan—it wasn't even noon, and frankly, you didn't look drunk, you looked spaced out."

"I got pretty trashed the night before," I said, hoping he'd buy it. "I was still drunk in the morning. I'm sorry, Albert, really, I was just out of it."

He sighed heavily. "You're not in some sort of trouble, are you?"

"I don't think so. Why?"

"If you are, maybe Carla and I can help."

"Thanks, but I'm okay," I lied.

He watched me a moment, weighing the validity of my response. "I don't want to pry, you understand, I'm just saying that if you're having issues, there's help available."

"I had a bad night," I said. "That's all."

"You sure that's all it is?"

"Yeah." I hated lying to him. He and Carla had been good to me and deserved better than that. But I didn't want to get them involved in whatever was happening. The less they knew the better. "Thanks for understanding, though. I'm really sorry I behaved that way."

Albert smiled, resumed sweeping, then abruptly stopped and said, "If you feel at some point you might want to talk about it, let me know, okay? I'm happy to help if I can. No pressure, just want you to know Carla and I are here if you need us."

"You're a good friend, Albert, thank you." I started for my cottage.

"Stan?"

I stopped, looked back. "Yeah?"

"You're not alone. It's important you know that."

With a halfhearted smile I nodded, waved and hurried back to my place.

I'd left the fans going but it was hotter than ever in there. I grabbed a beer from the fridge, ran it along my forehead and across the back of my neck, the can ice-cold against my flushed skin.

Christ, I thought, *the bastard's real.* Yet Albert said nothing about facial wounds, so could it have simply been me? If so, why did I have no memory of it? Could I have imagined the wounds and a true double really did knock on my door?

Why was this happening to me?

None of it seemed possible, much less plausible.

Suddenly, I had the feeling I was being watched. I did my best to shake it off. With my uncertainty and paranoia growing, I went to the bedroom. From the back of the top shelf, I pulled down a metal lockbox, then sat on the edge of my bed and let it rest across my lap. I stared at it a while, the greenish gray metal scratched and dented, the box held closed by a small padlock. I hadn't opened it in a long time, and until that moment I'd convinced myself I never would again. Those days were over. I didn't live that kind of life anymore. I went to work, came home, paid my bills and obeyed the law best I could. That was my life now, had been for some time.

I took hold of the padlock, my fingers moving deftly as I spun a combination I hadn't thought about or tried in several years. It worked on the first try. With a deep breath, I set the padlock aside and slowly lifted the lid.

Inside, wrapped in cloth, were a military-issue Beretta M9, a full 20-round clip, a new, unopened box of ammunition and a professional handgun cleaning kit in a compact carrying case. Alongside it lay a handheld police and fire scanner, a pair of lightweight black leather driving gloves, a Kubotan (a closequarter martial arts self-defense weapon roughly the width and length of a magic marker) scarred and worn from years of use, a pair of silver-plated brass knuckles, a stack of counterfeit driver's licenses from various states, and an old pair of sunglasses designed to be worn after dark to increase night vision and cut down on headlight glare.

I sipped my beer and stared at the items, a rush of memories returning to me. Even though I wished I didn't, I still found comfort in these things.

My phone began to ring, rescuing me, so I closed the box, put it on the bed and grabbed the phone from the nightstand. "Yeah?"

"Stan, it's me," a pleasant female voice said. "Sophie."

I closed my eyes, tried to reset. "Hey, Soph."

"You okay? Did I catch you at a bad time?"

"No, I was just in the middle of something but—no, it—it's fine."

"You sure? I can call back if you want."

"No, it's okay." I cleared my throat, had another swig of beer. "What's up?"

"I figured since we were both off for the weekend and I didn't have a whole lot going on that, well, maybe you might want to have that drink with me today."

I went to the window that looked out over the bluff and ocean beyond. A date was about the last thing on my radar, but I needed someone to talk to. I didn't know Sophie that well, but my instincts told me I could trust her. Years ago, those same instincts had kept me alive, and although they'd become a bit rusty since the days when I'd relied on such things, I still believed in them. But I was broke. "The thing is," I said, "I've got an unexpected problem with my finances."

"Don't worry about it. I'm asking you out, I'll foot the bill." She laughed in a way I envied, at once fierce and unencumbered. "Fair enough?"

"It's just that I had an issue with my account and it was emptied out."

"Were you robbed?"

"Sort of, I—yeah, but—well, not exactly." Christ, I sounded like an ass.

"Look," Sophie said, rescuing me yet again, "let's get together and we can talk about it over lunch. I'm starving, how about we meet over at the Beachside Inn?"

"Sure. Yes."

"Fifteen minutes?"

I could walk there in five, but she lived on the other side of town and was much farther away from the main drag than I was. "I'll meet you out front by the benches," I said.

"It's a date!"

I returned the phone to its cradle on the nightstand and then grabbed the lockbox and fastened and secured the padlock back in place. After shoving the box up on the closet shelf, I went into the kitchen and finished the rest of my beer.

Through the window, I saw Albert out on his deck practicing his tai chi routines. Carla, who was not at all athletic, was positioned at a nearby table reading a newspaper. In one of her typical Hawaiian shirts, khaki shorts, sandals and a cloth bush hat, she looked thoroughly bored with her boyfriend's moves, but occasionally glanced over at him and smiled fondly.

I envied them. They'd been together for years and were still happy and in love, and it showed. Their lives weren't perfect, but they'd obviously come much closer to what they'd set out looking for than I had.

At least things had been quiet for me for a long while. Now that was all changing. Just like years before, trouble had come looking for me. In the past I'd confronted it head-on, and for a time, even mastered it. But this was a different breed of trouble—I could feel it—and I was a lot older now.

I could only hope I was wiser too.

7

RISING. SLOWLY. GRADUALLY. RISING toward the surface of…of what?

The world is murky and wrapped in fog. A dull gray sheen moves and floats all around me like a ghost. And just beyond it, the dead ocean awaits. Still. Quiet. Evil. Something is coming I cannot yet see. I can only feel its spindly legs walking delicately across my flesh, little needles scraping the fine hairs along my arms, making me look, making me want to scratch and get them off me, away from me. They're suffocating me, blinding me.

The spiders.

They've come down from the ceiling. Or have I joined them up there, lying impossibly across the ceiling, covered in their fat bodies, caressed by their gangly legs?

Watched by their rows of soulless black eyes.

*　*　*

The Beachside Inn was aptly named, as it sat atop a large hill overlooking the longest stretch of public beach in Sunset. The Inn, an old renovated Victorian that in the 1870s had been the home of a local sea captain, featured country-style chic and offered lodging that came as close to posh as one was likely to find in a burg like Sunset. Their restaurant and bar was a lot nicer than most of the eateries around, relatively affordable and catered not only to the tourist trade but to locals as well. I'd been to the bar several times but hadn't eaten at the restaurant in a long time. I waited for Sophie at the benches in front, as I'd promised, hopeful I could shed my nightmares by the time she arrived.

She showed a few minutes later, on foot, having parked at a large lot farther down the street. With a bounce in her step I hadn't seen before, she bopped her way through the crowd of tourists and emerged with a wide smile and a little wave in my direction. I'd never seen Sophie in anything but her waitress uniform, so it took a moment to get used to her in a pair of white shorts, a sleeveless blouse and tennis shoes. A straw pocketbook hung over one shoulder, and she wore a baseball cap, her dark hair pulled into a ponytail that stuck out the back and bounced about playfully as she walked.

"Hey!" she said enthusiastically, eyes hidden behind the dark lenses of her black sunglasses.

I stood, forced my best smile and was just about to put my hand out when she leaned in, casually slung an arm around my shoulder and gave me a quick hug. "Good to see you," she said breathlessly.

Gently, I placed one hand on her back and gave it a pat. "You too."

We moved through a series of outdoor tables on the patio and into the restaurant, where a hostess sat us at a table not far from the bar.

It was busy but not loud, and we settled nicely into our little table in the corner. Once a waitress had brought us a couple glasses of water and two menus then moved away, Sophie removed her sunglasses and said, "God, I'm starving. I didn't have any breakfast. I'm having a lobster roll. I don't care what they're charging. Have you ever had them here? To die for!"

"I don't like lobster," I told her, bracing myself for the reaction that declaration always elicited.

"Huh?" She stared at me, mouth agape, as if I'd personally offended her. "What New Englander doesn't like lobster?"

"This one."

She shrugged, put her menu down. "So you're a cheap date then."

"Let's go with inexpensive."

Sophie laughed harder than seemed warranted, but I appreciated it. "How can you not like lobster? It's *so* good!"

"I don't like seafood."

"Okay, now you're just starting to piss me off."

I laughed, and it felt good.

"Hey, get whatever you want," she said. "Be happy, my treat."

"Sorry I'm hurting on funds, I—"

"No worries." Sophie gave me a quick pat on my arm, then sat back in her chair and sighed contentedly. "I can't remember the last time I went somewhere and someone waited on *me*, you know?"

"Yeah, I do actually. Been a while since I've been out to eat like this."

The waitress appeared again and Sophie ordered her lobster roll and a glass of chardonnay. I got a turkey club with fries and a beer.

"So, tell me what's going on," she said once we were alone again. "You weren't really clear on the phone. Did you get robbed or what?"

Although I left out the suicide attempt, with a great deal of hesitation, I told her everything else, from the loss of time after leaving work to the strange look-alike at my door both I and apparently Albert had encountered, the blank black business card, Duane's sighting of me, and my recent bad dreams. I felt absolutely ridiculous, but Sophie remained quiet and listened thoughtfully throughout. By the time I'd finished, our drinks had arrived.

Sophie sipped her wine. "You had a blackout, is that what you're saying?"

"I admit I drink more than I should, and I've experienced blackouts before, I'm not saying I haven't. But not like this. Maybe I've forgotten a conversation here or there, or lost little snippets of time, but I've never blacked out for an entire night."

"All right," she said, "let's put the whole doppelgänger thing aside for a sec. Granted, it's creepy, but let's focus first on your time and money loss."

"Okay."

"What's the last thing you remember Thursday night?"

"Leaving work."

"You don't remember anything else?"

I thought a moment, trying hard as I could to bring up some sort of memory. "I remember punching out and leaving. I remember walking out of the diner and turning toward home. I remember briefly walking along the drag."

"And then?"

"Nothing."

"What's your next memory?"

"Waking up Friday morning with one of the worst hangovers I'd ever had, and being really groggy. Hazy, you know?"

"Having never had a hangover myself," Sophie said, twisting her face into a comical expression, "I'll just have to imagine what it was like."

I sipped my beer. Maybe I was no better than my old man. Maybe I was just a drunk like him, not homeless and living outside like Duane, but still a drunk and a bum, a loser haunted by bad dreams in a slowly dying mind. Who else had blackouts to that level?

"All joking aside," Sophie said, holding her wineglass with both hands and leaning forward on the table so she could address me in a softer voice. "Sometimes I drink more than I should too. Hell, I still smoke weed on a regular basis, so who am I to judge you or anyone else? But Stan, if you're experiencing blackouts to this degree, it's a good indication that it's time to get some help."

"If I really did black out, then you're right. But it just doesn't add up."

"Okay, what am I missing?"

"I left work at eleven," I explained. "The next time I know for sure where I was is an hour and thirty-six minutes later when I appear at the ATM and empty my account. Now, I saw that video twice, it was very clear and easy to see. I didn't look drunk in it. I looked a little off, maybe, but not drunk."

"Off how?"

"Just not myself, I guess. Distracted."

"And it was definitely you? No way it could have been someone else?"

"No. Not unless…"

"You have a double running around, and I think we can rule that out. But we'll get to that. Right now let's assume it was you then. You have no idea where you were from eleven until twelve thirty-six?"

"Right."

"And you're saying you weren't drunk when you took the money out?"

"I didn't look drunk, no."

"What happens next?"

"Fourteen minutes later my buddy Duane sees me at twelve fifty. I'm headed toward home at that point."

"And did Duane think you were drunk at that time?"

"He said he waved to me and I just looked at him and kept walking, which is something I'd never do. He never said I looked drunk, though."

"But you said he was drunk himself."

I nodded.

Sophie thought for a moment, staring into her white wine. "And at some point you somehow get hold of a blank black business card."

"Apparently."

"But was this before or after you went home?"

"I have no memory of any of this, so I can't be sure, but the odds that I'd go home that late and then turn around and go back out again are slim to none."

"I ask this without judgment. Do you do any drugs, Stan?"

"No."

"It's cool, like I say, I smoke pot."

"Haven't done drugs in years. Last time I even smoked weed I was in my twenties."

"What about prescription drugs?"

"I have some pain pills but I haven't taken them in a while."

"And you didn't hurt yourself? You didn't fall, hit your head or have some sort of medical episode or something?"

I shook my head no, then had another sip of beer.

She looked deep into my eyes. Not to flirt, but to gauge the validity of my responses. "Okay," she said softly. "Was there any indication you'd driven your car that night?"

"No. I walked to and home from work."

"If we assume you weren't drunk when you were at the ATM, then it wasn't a blackout—at least not at that point—that caused you to forget everything, but something else."

"Like what?"

"Damned if I know. But think about it. You leave work and go somewhere other than home. Then you wind up back on the drag, where you decide to go to the ATM for some reason and empty out your bank account. After that, you're walking home and seen by Duane, something you have no memory of either. You go home and drink yourself into oblivion, meaning unless someone broke into your cottage and stole the cash from you while you were passed out, you lost or spent the money prior, during the missing time."

"Unless I went back out that night, which is unlikely, I spent or lost that money between twelve thirty-six when I took it out, and twelve fifty when Duane saw me. Or in the handful of remaining minutes it took me to get home from where he saw me."

"I don't know this Duane person, but he wouldn't have taken it, right?"

"He wouldn't steal from me. And I don't know how he could without my knowing it anyway."

"What if you were in some sort of state or something? Drugged, let's say."

"Drugged?"

"Have you given that any thought?"

"Someone drugging me?"

"It happens. Women get roofied all the time. Why not a guy?"

A chill passed through me. I chalked it up to the air-conditioning in the restaurant. Could someone have slipped me something somehow and then taken advantage of me, convinced me in some altered state to empty my bank account?

"Thing is, at the ATM, I do look off but not anywhere near as drugged out as I'd have to be for someone to convince me to do that."

"Is there any other reason you might've taken the money out?"

"No, it was every dime I had, Soph."

"You're totally broke?"

"Wiped out."

She reached over to the vacant chair next to her where she'd put her purse and pulled it into her lap. "I don't have a lot," she said, rummaging through it before coming up with a wallet. "Because I'm a broke-ass bitch like yourself, but I do have a little extra. I've got some cash on me. I can pay for lunch with my debit card."

"No," I said. "I—"

"Payday's a week away. You can't be without money for an entire week."

"It's not your problem, I can't take money from you, I—"

"Shush." She placed a small stack of cash on the table and slid it over to me. "It's only a hundred bucks, but that should get you through until your next check."

"Sophie—"

"Take it."

"I can't."

"I want you to have it. Besides, it's just a loan."

"Sophie, I *can't*."

"Take it and shut the hell up, you're giving me a headache." She wagged a finger at me as if reprimanding a child. "I'm a mother, don't mess with me. We know how to make your life miserable if we want to, trust me. Now take it. Pay me back when you can, all right?"

"That's not what any of this was about."

"I know that," she said, returning her things to her purse. "Don't you think I know that? For Christ's sake, Stan, we're friends. Don't make a big deal about it."

Before I could object any further, the waitress appeared with our lunches. I put the cash in my pocket if for no other reason than I didn't want her to see it.

For the next half hour or so, we ate and drank and chatted about other, more pleasant things. I couldn't remember the last time I had such a nice time, or even came close to allowing myself one. The mystery of what had happened continued to hang over everything like the dark cloud it was, but for just a little while we did our best to ignore it.

After we finished eating, we left the Beachside Inn and walked over to an ice-cream place a block away. A local institution, it had existed in the same location in one form or another since the early 1950s, and although it had been renovated and changed owners numerous times, it maintained the look, feel and charm of an ice-cream parlor from yesteryear.

The beaches were so crowded there was no point in going anywhere near them, so we took our ice cream cones and walked the drag and surrounding area, the cries from the waterpark and the plethora of smells, sights and other sounds of the summer hotspot we called home alive all around us.

By midafternoon we found ourselves at the outskirts of the band shell, where a local pop group was banging out a subpar version of an old Blondie tune. Several people were scattered about the large lawn on blankets and such, having picnics or just relaxing and taking in the music and the beautiful day.

We sat on a bench far enough from the stage that we could still have a conversation. I'd worked with Sophie for nearly a year, but this was the first time I'd really noticed her in anything but a casual way. She'd suddenly become this whole person in a matter of minutes, and the more of herself she revealed to me and the better I got to know her, the more I liked what I saw and heard. Though cynical at times, well grounded and in possession of a very dry wit, there was also an abandon and youthful enthusiasm to her I envied. But what was perhaps the most appealing was the maturity and grace that existed alongside the rest. Her contradictions were more than fascinating. They actually complemented her. I hadn't been on a date, if that's what this was, in years, much less part of a relationship, and while it still felt somewhat foreign and awkward to me, I was also remarkably comfortable in Sophie's presence. She was safe, in a sense, and that felt good. *She* felt good. It was nice to be in the company of a woman I liked and found attractive, and who, for some ungodly reason, apparently had the same attraction to me. I'd almost forgotten what any of that was like.

"I've been thinking about that guy at your door," she said rather suddenly.

We hadn't discussed anything more about what had happened since lunch, and I was a bit surprised she'd returned to the topic. I didn't want to involve her in any real sense, I'd just needed to vent.

Sophie dug a pack of cigarettes and a lighter from her purse. "I'm trying to see if I can come up with a connection between him and the lost time."

"Do you think they're related?"

"Do you?"

"I don't know. Probably. Little too coincidental not to be, no?"

She tapped the pack until a single cigarette slid partially free of the others. "And he really looked just like you?"

"Yeah, except for the wounds on his face. But then again, Albert never mentioned that, so maybe I was the only who saw them. It's crazy, I know."

With my apprehension and discomfort growing, I looked out at the people on the lawn, in the seats, on the street, everyone moving all around us. He could be out there anywhere, I thought, or nowhere at all, just a figment of my exhausted mind, a phantom from a dark dream.

"The times correspond," Sophie said. "Albert sees whoever this is and then moments later he knocks on your door, right? So whoever he is, he obviously knows where to find you, and there must be some point to his being there."

A nice breeze blew in off the ocean. "If he even exists at all."

"Could you have imagined him, or maybe dreamed him? Maybe Albert saw you, not some double, and you were out of it again and didn't realize or remember."

"I guess, I—I don't know. Been having a lot of bad dreams lately."

Sophie plucked the cigarette free and rolled it into the corner of her mouth, letting it dangle there, unlit. "Time will tell. It always does."

Despite it all, I felt myself smile. "You should've been a detective."

"Nah," she said, lighting her cigarette through a grin. "I just read a lot of crime and mystery novels. I know, awesome, right? I drink too much wine, live with my cat and substitute paperbacks for relationships. I guess now's not the right time to bring up my obsession with interpretive dance, huh?"

A child suddenly screeched, having fallen nearby and skinned his knee. His mother picked him up and comforted him as his father looked on with concern.

"If it wasn't you, and this guy exists," Sophie said, considering the distraction only long enough to determine the child was fine, "maybe he just strongly resembles you, and given your state of mind at the time, you saw more than was really there."

"Albert did say I had a sweatshirt on with the hood up."

"In this weather? Well, maybe he didn't really get as good a look at this guy as he thought then, and mistakenly assumed it was you."

"I don't know who else it could've been," I said, staring at the ground. "At the risk of sounding pathetic, I don't know a lot of people, don't really have any friends. Except for Duane and maybe Albert and Carla."

Sophie lowered her sunglasses long enough to playfully glare at me.

"And you," I added.

"And you say you looked away and he was gone?"

"Like he'd never been there."

We were quiet a while.

The band began butchering James Taylor's "Shower the People," the lead singer dramatically over-stylizing the lyrics. I looked at Sophie and made a face.

"I know, right? It's like a bad *SNL* skit." She took a drag on her cigarette. "I'm having a really nice time, though."

"Me too."

"You want to get out of here?"

"I should probably get home."

"Big plans for tonight?"

"Well no, but—"

"Want to come back to my place for a bit and hang out?" She took another drag, then dropped the cigarette to the ground and stepped on it. "I have cookies. Good ones."

"We talking chocolate chip or…?"

"Homemade." She stood up. "Come on, it'll be fun. You can meet Balthazar."

"I'd like to," I said softly. "I really would."

"But?"

"With all this shit going on, I'm not sure that's a good idea."

"I'm a big girl. I can take care of myself."

"I have no doubt about that. I just…"

She smiled. "Jesus, Stan, relax. I just invited you back to my place to chill for a while, I'm not asking you to marry me."

Despite her humorous tone, I could feel her pain lurking just beneath the surface. I knew it well because it lived in me too. We were both broken and lonely. And we were both tired of it.

"Just thought it might be fun to spend an evening with someone that's not my cat. I mean, Balthazar's the bomb and I love him to death, but he's not much of a conversationalist. Also, his breath smells like fish and he hacks up hairballs that look like turds. So, you know, he's got that going for him." She selfconsciously straightened her hair. "You want to come hang out for a while, I'd love to have you. If not, that's cool too, I can drop you off at home. Up to you."

I wished she weren't wearing sunglasses. I wanted to see her eyes. "Do you really have cookies?"

"Oh I've got cookies, baby."

What the hell, I thought. *I didn't want to go home anyway.*

8

WHEN I WAS SEVEN years old, I got an action figure for Christmas. It wasn't a G.I. Joe or a name figure like that, just a standard doll in an army uniform, but I loved it and carried it around with me everywhere, played with it all the time and pretended to be a soldier along with him, like in the movies I'd seen. There was a button on his chest, and if pushed, in a melodramatic voice he'd say an assortment of things like, "*Attack!*" or "*Storm the beach!*" or "*Enemy fire, take cover!*" It was without question the coolest toy I'd ever had. A few weeks after I got it, my father came home drunk and found me sitting on the floor in the den reading one of my comic books. My action figure lay next to me. Without a word, he grabbed it and tore it apart, throwing the pieces to the floor once he'd finished. I just sat there looking up at him, stunned and confused as to why he would do such a thing.

"What do you think about that, you little prick?" he said, slurring his words to the point that he drooled a long string of spittle from his bottom lip without seeming to realize it. "So sick of hearing that thing yak all the time. I told your mother not to get it, but she never listens.

Just like you, she's too goddamn busy disrespecting me to fucking *listen*."

Despite my best efforts, I couldn't prevent tears from filling my eyes, so I looked down at the floor in the hopes my father wouldn't realize I was crying.

"Look at me when I'm talking to you, boy!"

Next thing I knew, he had a handful of my hair and was pulling me up onto my feet, spinning me around and slapping me in the face with his free hand.

My mother appeared from the kitchen, pleading with him to stop.

He let me go and beat her instead. When I tried to help her, he beat me too.

A few days later, while attending a relative's birthday party, we all posed together for a family photograph. That same photo still hung on a wall in my father's house, but I remembered looking at it as a kid and how we all seemed so happy in it. My father particularly, had a big wide smile, one arm around my mother, the other around me. And my mother and I were smiling too, like all was right with the world with our happy little family. If I looked closely enough, I could see the heavy makeup around my mother's eyes, covering the bruises my father's fists had left in their wake.

Liars. We were all liars.

The past melted and dripped away like blood, replaced by a photograph of Sophie and her two kids when they were younger. The picture sat in a frame on the shelf of a bookcase in her living room, amidst countless books and knickknacks.

"I love that picture," she said, moving toward me from the kitchen, a drink in one hand and a glass of wine in the other.

She looked different. Not just younger, but different somehow. "It's nice."

"Yeah." She gazed at it longingly. "Look at my babies, so little back then."

I smiled.

She handed me my drink. "I believe you ordered the Jack on the rocks."

"Thanks."

We moved over to a small couch and sat down. Sophie's apartment was modest but nice, consisting of a living room, kitchenette area and a single bedroom. Located in a small building on the far side of town, a good distance from the main drag and all the tourists, it was quieter here, a working-class, predominantly residential neighborhood of mostly older houses that had been converted into apartments. She'd been nothing but accommodating, but I was still getting used to spending time with her outside of work. It was strange to be in her living space, exposed to this part of her life that had been private until now, and I felt like an intruder.

"What were you thinking about just now?" she asked. "You looked intense."

"Bad times," I said, sipping my drink. "Long time ago."

"We've all had them." She pulled her legs up under her and leaned against the back of the couch, turning so she was facing me. "Life in the neighborhood we lived in when I was a kid wasn't exactly bliss."

"You got out early though, right?"

"Yeah, we moved up here when I was still young." Sophie had some wine, but suddenly seemed uncomfortable. "I have an older brother that wasn't so lucky. Did ten years in Walpole, but he got transferred to medium-security back in ninety-six. Been up to Concord ever since."

"When's he getting out?" I asked.

"He's not."

"I'm sorry."

"He wasn't a bad guy. Tough neighborhood, got in with the wrong crowd."

"I understand."

"Yeah, you do, don't you?" Her eyes searched mine now. "He was part of a crew that hit an armored car. One of the security guards decided to be a hero, started a shootout and wound up dead. My brother was the shooter. They gave him two lifetimes and then some. I used to go visit him all the time, but after a couple years he asked me to stop. I didn't want to but it was just too hard for him. Haven't seen my brother in years."

"That's rough."

I felt peculiar discussing such things because I'd never told anyone about my past and hadn't planned to tell her either. But for some reason it seemed like the right thing to do, like it might provide me with release, a way of shaking off some of the heavy chains that had hung around my neck for so long.

"I've never done prison time," I confessed, "but I did a couple short stints in jail when I was younger. Nothing too serious, petty stuff, but I fell into that life for a while too. Mean streets, you know? And sometimes my home life was even worse."

She gave a mischievous smile. "Were you really in sales like you said?"

"I was." I had another swallow of Jack. I was going to need it. "When I was younger, I got into some bad shit, and same as your brother, ran with a bad crowd. Drugs, violence, petty crimes, the whole nine, and it got to a point where things were either going to ratchet up and get really serious, or I was going to go another way. A few of us started working for a local loan shark and bookie, mostly collecting money and, when necessary, providing muscle. I was sure my life would never be anything but what it already was. I'd be a criminal, just like all my friends. Then I met Linda—my ex-wife—and everything changed."

"Wow." Sophie tossed her hair to one side and let her cheek rest against the palm of her hand. "She must've been really special."

"She was." I pushed away fond memories, along with the darker ones that always followed. "For the first time it seemed possible that I could have a regular life, you know? I didn't come from much. My father was a sadistic drunk that beat the shit out of my mother and me every chance he got. I hated the sonofabitch. Still do. My mother…well…I loved her. She died when I was a teenager. Liver issues due to alcoholism. She was a sweet woman, a good woman, but a limited and weak woman. Whatever light she had in her he snuffed out long before that bum liver ever got hold of her. Wasn't much left for me, so hope wasn't exactly a reality in my world. When I met Linda, I wasn't sure what to make of it. I'd never seen salvation before, I didn't know what it was."

Across from us, sitting along the back of a comfortable chair, her cat Balthazar watched us with disinterest, teetering between consciousness and a nap.

"I quit everything," I continued. "Went straight. We got married and I landed a regular job. Nobody could believe it, but I was all in. I even quit drinking."

"But then?"

"We had a deal, Linda and me. I promised to never go back to the booze and to never have anything to do with the life I'd led before I met her."

"What'd she promise?"

"To love me forever if I did." I took a drink. "I stuck to it for a long time, and we had some good years. Then…"

The words caught in my throat, and I wasn't sure I could continue. I wanted to tell Sophie everything, it felt good to finally be talking about these things after all these years, but what was coming next was so difficult I rarely allowed myself to think of it, much less voice it.

"It's okay," she said, touching my arm with her free hand. "It is. It's okay."

This time I searched her eyes. She was right. It was okay.

"We started a family," I said.

Visions flooded my mind. I closed my eyes in the hope of warding them off but they only got worse. My heart raced, and I suddenly felt queasy. "I'm sorry."

Sophie's hand was still on my arm. She slid it down onto my hand and gently stroked it. "Don't be," she said softly.

A waterfall of emotions washed over me, memories I hadn't had in years crashing down on me like waves. My grip on the glass tightened. "We had a little girl," I said. "Most amazing thing I've ever seen, I—I couldn't believe I'd had a part in making something so perfect."

Sophie nodded her understanding in a way only another parent could.

"But when I held that little girl in my arms and she looked up at me with those big eyes, I knew right then the rest of my life was going to be about loving her and keeping her safe and giving her the best life I possibly could. All the pain and horror my father had inflicted on me was something she'd never know." I cleared my throat, choking on the emotion. "Things were so good. I didn't even know happiness like that existed until…" I stopped short of saying my daughter's name. I hadn't spoken it in a very long time. "She was a good kid."

Sophie had another sip of wine but kept rubbing my hand.

"Everything was perfect," I continued. "And then she got sick. Leukemia. She was dead less than two years later. She was five when we buried her."

"God, Stan," Sophie said, just above a whisper. "I'm so sorry."

"Do you have any idea what it's like to watch your child die, slowly, a little more each day, and there's not a goddamn thing you can do about it?"

"Thankfully, no, I don't."

I forced myself to look at her. I wasn't the only one with tears in my eyes. "I was her father, her daddy. I was supposed to fix it, to make it all better, and I couldn't. I couldn't do a fucking thing. At first the horror of it all actually brought Linda and me closer together. But that was short-term. Things went to shit after that. I couldn't handle what had happened and I started drinking again. Promise number one broken. Within a few months I'd lost my job and was running around with a lot of the old crowd, spending time in the old neighborhood again and doing things I shouldn't have been doing. Promise two broken. Linda put up with it for a while, but when we lost the house, well, by that time she'd already met somebody else. Who could blame her?" I pawed at my eyes until they'd dried, then I powered down the rest of my drink and put the glass on the coffee table. "I lost everything. So I headed out to California for a while, bummed around out west for a few years, trying to figure out what the hell to do with myself and bouncing from one nowhere job to the next. Didn't think I'd ever come back, but I did. Wound up in Sunset a few years ago. Worked a bunch of different jobs around town until I landed at the diner almost a year ago. Been there ever since."

Sophie was quiet. She remained deep in thought, but said nothing.

"That's my story," I said a moment later. "I wish it was something better, but there it is."

"What was her name?" she asked. "Your daughter, what was her name?"

"You don't want any part of this, Sophie, I'm a fucking train wreck. I'm a shell, you understand? There's nothing left worth being around or getting to know any better than you already have."

"What was her name?" she pressed, eyes brimming with tears.

I swallowed hard, felt my body tremble. "Olivia."

The moment her name left my lips I bowed my head, ashamed at the tears filling my eyes again. I wanted to run, to get out of there and away from everything and everyone. I wanted another drink. I wanted lots of drinks. So many goddamn drinks I wouldn't feel anything ever again.

I started to get up but Sophie grabbed hold of me and pulled me back down, throwing herself against me and wrapping me in a hug, her mouth next to my ear and whispering to me that everything was all right. Nuzzled up against her, she smelled like cologne and baby powder, her body soft and warm. I hadn't been that close to a woman in a long time, and I felt like a nervous schoolkid fumbling around on his first date. The emotion of the moment and everything talking about the past had brought up in me was too much. To segue right into sex didn't seem possible.

"Sophie—" I gasped, realizing only then that my heart was racing and my breathing had become heavy.

She silenced me by pressing her lips against mine.

As our tongues met, I tasted sweet traces of wine in her mouth mixed with the harshness of tobacco. Pulling her closer, I wrapped my arms around her as she slowly fell onto her back, bringing me with her. Once she lay on the cushions and I'd slid on top of her, she kicked her sandals off, then wrapped her legs around me, locking her ankles across the small of my back and pulling me in tighter against her.

We kissed for what seemed like hours, our hands running across each other's bodies and our passion and lust growing stronger and stronger until it bordered on unbearable.

"Bedroom?" I asked as I came up for air.

Sophie was panting heavily, and as she'd removed the baseball cap when we first got there, the rubber band holding her ponytail in place had fallen free and her hair lay strewn across her face in a mess, giving her a wild, feral look. "Yeah," she said breathlessly. "Definitely."

But the break gave me a moment to think and consider what we were doing.

"Wait," I said, crawling off and stumbling away. "This isn't a good idea."

She rolled onto her side, swung her legs around to the floor and pushed herself up into a sitting position. Pulling her hair out of her face, she dropped it behind her shoulders and said, "Okay."

I was embarrassed by the erection tenting my pants but there wasn't much I could do about it. "Sophie, it's just that I…"

She had no intention of saving me this time.

I wanted to pace but was having enough trouble walking so I did my best to pull off a casually unaffected pose. "You're amazing," I said. "And I like you a lot, I really do. But I don't know if I can do this."

"Maybe if you could just stop hating yourself so much."

"I can barely take care of myself."

"When did I ask you to take care of me?" She reached over to the coffee table and retrieved her cigarettes and lighter. "You're making this a lot harder than it needs to be."

"I'm sorry." I stood there like a moron, unsure of what else to say.

She lit a cigarette, took a hungry drag and then another. "It's cool," she finally said, her breathing back under control. "I just thought— shit, I don't know what I thought—but when you opened up to me like that, it was incredibly powerful and I let it—sorry, I shouldn't have thrown myself at you like that."

"I'm flattered beyond belief."

She exhaled smoke from her nostrils. "I'm confused then. Do you have some sort of no-fucking-people-you-work-with policy or some-thing?"

"That's usually a good idea, but no, it's nothing like that."

She laughed lightly.

"What?"

"You're so formal sometimes, it's really goofy."

"Sorry."

"I actually think it's kind of cute."

"I'm sorry," I said again.

"Yeah, I heard you the first time." Sophie lay back into the couch and smoked her cigarette. "Let's just forget any of this ever happened, okay? You want me to run you home?"

"No."

"It's been a long time, hasn't it?"

I nodded.

"Me too."

"The idea of starting something again isn't—Sophie, it's not like we picked each other up in a bar. We know each other, we—we're friends—and I—I'm not somebody you should get involved with, trust me."

She grinned, the cigarette held between her lips. "Maybe I'm somebody *you* shouldn't get involved with. Ever think of that?"

There was something about her slumped down into the cushions of that couch, her legs open and her clothes disheveled, the cigarette hanging from her mouth. "You some kind of bad girl?"

She arched an eyebrow. "Maybe."

"I like being friends with you," I said awkwardly. "And I don't want to screw that up for a few minutes in the sack."

"So I'm missing out on the best forty-seven seconds of my life, is that it?"

"A solid thirty to thirty-five anyway."

She barked out a laugh and I felt valuable. "You could still stay." With one more quick drag on her cigarette, she sat forward and crushed the butt out in the ashtray. "We can hang out, fire up some microwave popcorn and watch a movie or something really original like that. Maybe later, we could lay down a while, I'll drive you home in the morning. Doesn't have to get complicated. We can just snuggle. It'd be nice to feel someone next to me in the dark. I've almost forgotten what that's like. No offense, Balthazar."

The cat yawned and looked away, thoroughly unamused.

I moved to the nearest window. The sun was low in the sky. Night was still a few hours off, but it was on its way, daylight was dying. For the first time, I was glad I'd avoided the gallows. All that time preparing, convincing myself suicide was the right thing to do, the only alternative, the one chance I had at peace and quieting the storms inside me. Until that moment I was convinced I'd become incapable of feeling much of anything besides pain. But there they were again, those old feelings whispering to me that maybe there *was* a point to my shattered life. And it was worth sticking around for.

"Stan?"

I turned from the window and looked back at Sophie, certain now that there was nowhere else I wanted to be.

"What do you think?" she asked.

"I think I was promised cookies."

9

NIGHT. THE STREET IS *dark and deserted. It's a beautiful night, with a sky full of stars, but there is something wrong. I can feel it creeping closer, stalking me like prey. I've been in dangerous situations before and can handle myself, but on this night I know fear. On this night the Devil lives and breathes.*

And he's getting closer.

A car appears, turns at the corner, then rolls slowly up alongside me. Someone says something unintelligible from inside the car, the voice deep and garbled. Through the partially open window I see a silhouette but cannot make out any detail.

And then someone's approaching on foot, moving along the sidewalk and walking right toward me. A man. I can only see part of his face in the darkness.

There is someone...something...behind me. I can feel its presence.

As I turn, a face explodes from the darkness and lunges for me. A demon, a witch—stark and pallid, the face powdered white but for a single black stripe that runs down its middle—the eyes painted blood-red, the whites feral and glassy and diseased. Long black hair drapes either side of it, a tangle of beads and feathers and strips of cloth and leather dangling from it like ornaments.

The demon blows into its open palm, dispersing a cloud of mist that sprays my face and blinds me. I stagger back as a nauseating taste coats the inside of my mouth.

And then I'm falling, spiraling down.

Down into Hell...

* * *

I opened my eyes, let them adjust to the darkness, and then, without moving, looked to the right, across the bed and in the direction of the door. It was closed. Panning my eyes back across the bedroom, I covered the entire area until I was satisfied we were alone.

Somewhere, at the very edge of my memory...something...but before I could grab hold of it, the memory—or whatever it was—slipped free, drifting away like smoke spiraling from a snuffed candle. In its wake, only fear.

The old air-conditioner in the window rattled and hummed noisily, making it difficult to hear much of anything else, but in those first moments when I'd come awake, I swore I'd heard something in the other room. I told myself it was only the nightmare that had spooked me, but I lay still a while and listened anyway.

The alarm clock on the nightstand read: 11:47. We'd been asleep just under an hour. Sophie lay next to me on her back, mouth open as she snored quietly. We lay atop the sheets and comforter, and except for our shoes, remained fully clothed.

I rolled onto my side so I could better see over her. A narrow band of light shone beneath the bottom of the door. Hadn't Sophie turned everything off when we went to bed? I thought so but couldn't be sure. Sitting up, I brought my feet to the floor and pushed them into my sneakers.

Just as I was about to go check the rest of the apartment, I was instinctually drawn to the long double windows along the back wall of the bedroom. Without turning on a light, I approached them and looked out at the night. A pale yellow star caught my eye. *Saturn,* I thought, though I had no idea how I knew that or even if I was correct. And yet, there was something about that realization that left me both confused and anxious. It was unsettling, and suddenly I wanted nothing more than to run, to get away from there, away from that *thing* sparkling in the dark sky, but the enormous full moon hanging before me demanded attention, brilliant and surreal, its glow casting eerie specters of ghostly iridescent light along the street.

I looked to the building directly across the way. It was dark and quiet. On the sidewalk out front an array of trash cans had been left near the curb, along with a pile of green plastic bags bulging with refuse.

And then I noticed something else.

Across the street, a dark form stood watching Sophie's apartment.

I stepped to the side of the windows. Reminding me it was still there, the fear my nightmare had left behind slithered closer and coiled deep inside me, its conversion to the world of the living complete. I peered around the edge of the window casing until I could see the man again. Partially concealed in shadows, for several minutes he stood perfectly still, staring up at the apartment. Without altering my position, I did my best to look up then down the block, but far as I could tell, the man was alone.

I didn't want to frighten Sophie, so I rounded the bed quietly as I could and slipped out, closing the bedroom door behind me.

In the light of the other room, I saw that a lamp had been left on but there was no one else in the apartment and nothing out of the ordinary. Opening the front door, then closing it softly behind me, I moved along a short hallway, then down a flight of stairs until I'd reached the foyer at the entrance to the building. I could no longer make out the man across the street, as the shadows from this vantage point were too thick, but the foyer was dark so I knew he probably couldn't see me either.

Outside, the air was thick and hot, the night deathly quiet.

Fast as I could, I crossed the street and closed on the area where I'd seen the man, but no one was there. Already dripping with perspiration, I checked the alley between the buildings.

At the far mouth of the alley, a shadow slipped around the corner and disappeared from view. I hurried after it, moving quickly but not running so my footfalls wouldn't make too much noise.

When I reached the end of the alley, I stopped, leaned against the corner of the building and peered at the street beyond.

The man was moving toward a small parking lot across the street.

I followed, this time breaking into a run.

He heard me coming and looked behind him, visibly surprised to find me bearing down on him. Scruffy, with small rodent-like eyes, the man held his hands up like this might stop me. "Hey, what—what's up?" he muttered.

Only a few feet away from him now, I came to a stop. "Who are you?" I asked.

"Who are *you*?" He arched an eyebrow. "Why you running up on me, bro?"

Although I was certain I'd never seen the man before, there was something about him that bothered me. Masking it best I could, I remained where I was. I couldn't be certain this was the same man I'd seen watching Sophie's building but who else would be out on the street this late in such an otherwise quiet, residential neighborhood?

But for a nearby streetlight, I couldn't see him that well, so I took a step closer. Thin, with pockmarked skin, he was clad in cheap polyester dress slacks, black cowboy boots and a bowling shirt. A wallet in his back pocket was attached to a thin chain that dangled down to his thigh. He needed a shave, and his slick black hair was styled with pomade into a comical-looking pompadour. "What are you doing out here?" I asked.

"You the neighborhood watch or some shit?" He grinned and winked at me like we were old friends. His was the drawn, bleary-eyed and emaciated look of a longtime alcoholic and drug abuser, and his hands, wrists and arms were littered with numerous tattoos, mostly the kind of ink one obtained in prison. "Out for a saunter, daddy, what's the problem?"

"This time of night?"

He gave a little laugh and sized me up without subtlety. "What'd you want?"

"Why were you watching the building?"

"What building?"

"Are you following me?"

"Fuck you talking about? *You* come up on *me*, brother."

"Why were you watching the building?"

He offered his best poker face. "I don't know what you're talking about, man." He turned and started for the parking lot. "Peace."

"Hold up," I said.

He did, but began fidgeting about nervously. "Come on, big daddy, I don't want no heat, all right?"

"You were watching the building," I said. "And you're following me. Why?"

He feigned indifference and lit a cigarette, cupping the flame with his hand even though there wasn't any wind. "You a little paranoid or something?"

"Answer the question."

He looked everywhere but directly at me. "Hell's wrong with you, bro? I didn't do nothing, I—shit—I don't even know you. Why you hassling me?"

"Who are you?"

"I'm me."

"What's your name, wise-ass?"

He took a deep drag on his cigarette, exhaled through his nose. "The name's Chic, all right? What's it to you, tough guy?"

"What are you doing out here, *Chic*?"

"Look, you go your way, I go mine. It's all roses, dig?"

I felt something dark within me coming alive for the first time in years. "Don't make me ask you again."

"Or what?"

I stared at him but said nothing.

"Yeah, that's what I figured." He flicked the cigarette at me, and as it bounced off my chest in a spray of sparks, he walked away.

He'd made it two steps before I grabbed him by the shoulder and spun him back around. He staggered, a bit off-balance, but quickly righted himself and pulled something from his pocket. As he thrust his hand toward me, a blade snapped into view with a loud click, just inches from my face.

"Back off!" he spat.

I did, raising my hands. "Take it easy."

"I'm always easy, boss." Chic stood his ground, brimming with new-found confidence, the blade still hovering right near my face. "But don't put your hands on me again, you got it?"

I snatched his wrist, turned it until he'd dropped the knife, then jammed my forearm into his throat and walked him back to the side of the nearest building, slamming him against it with enough force to let him know things could get a lot worse for him if that's how I decided to play it.

"Okay, pally," he gasped. "O-Okay!"

Holding him in place with one hand, I reached down and yanked his wallet free with the other. The cheap chain snapped and swung away. I released him, then picked up his knife, closed the blade and handed it back to him. "Put your toy away like a good boy or I'll stab it so far up your ass you'll choke on it."

Chic returned the switchblade to his pocket but was more concerned with his wallet. "What, you gonna rob me now, man?"

He stepped off the wall but I pushed him back into it.

I flipped open the wallet, saw a driver's license showcasing his homely mug and a home address listed in Brockton. In a slot just beneath it was a blank black business card, just like the one I had. My heart dropped but I maintained my composure. "Brockton's a good forty, forty-five minutes from here," I said. "What are you doing in Sunset?"

Chic smiled wide. One of his front teeth was gold. "You need to let me glide, Clyde, before you get us both killed. You dig?"

"No, I don't dig. I don't *dig* at all."

He laughed but there was no humor in it. It had a horrible edge, sick and depraved and awful. "You don't want to start acting the fool with me, brother man."

I took a step closer to him. "You gonna make me take this where it doesn't need to go, Chic?"

The smile vanished. His beady eyes shifted about. "Come on, man."

"What do you want with me?" I asked. "Why you following me?"

"Who said I was following you? Maybe I was casing the joint. Maybe I'm out for a midnight stroll and got lost. Maybe I'm sleepwalking. Maybe you need to blow it out your poop hole 'cause it ain't none of your beeswax *what* I'm doing. Hate to break it to you, baby, but not everything's about you."

I pulled the black card from his wallet, held it up. "What's this?"

"Never seen it before."

"Oh, it's not yours? I didn't just pull it out your wallet right in front of you?"

He shrugged.

"Then I guess you won't mind if I hang on to it," I said.

"I don't give a shit what you do, Scooter."

He was bluffing and we both knew it, but I slipped the card into my pocket anyway.

"We done, boss?" he asked.

I'd known dozens of guys like Chic back in the day. The only way to reach his kind was to ratchet up the violence. If I hurt him, he'd tell me whatever I wanted to know. Luckily for him, I wasn't prepared to take it to that level. Not here. Not now. Not yet.

"Go," I said.

"Can I get my wallet back?"

I pulled his license, stuck it in my pocket along with the card, then tossed him the wallet.

"You serious? You keeping my ID, bro?" Chic was trying to play it cool but was clearly coming out of his skin. "I need my license, dude."

"I'll see you real soon," I told him. "Give it back to you then."

Barely containing his panic, he shuffled his feet and nervously scratched at the stubble along his throat. "This is bullshit, you—you don't wanna be—"

"Get out of my sight." I cocked my head toward the parking lot.

Shaking his head, he walked to his vehicle, a beatup windowless red van that looked like something someone who abducted children might drive.

Chic pulled out and drove off, leaving me standing on the sidewalk in the middle of the night. I couldn't be sure of anything anymore.

But I knew now what needed to be done.

10

WHEN I GOT BACK to Sophie's apartment, I found her awake and pacing about nervously. "What's going on? Why were you outside at this hour?"

"It's okay," I said, closing the door behind me.

"I woke up and heard you leaving," she explained. "Then I saw you out the window running across the street and—"

"Soph, there was someone out there. He was watching the apartment."

She looked at me like I was crazy. "What?"

"There was a man outside, across the street. He was watching the apartment. This apartment." Despite the cool air in the room, I was pouring sweat. I wiped my face with the back of my hand and as I swung my arm back around I inadvertently knocked over a glass vase full of flowers from a small table near the door. "Shit, sorry." I bent down and started to clean it up.

"Leave it," Sophie said, grabbing the wall phone in the kitchen. "I'll get it. I need to know what—Stan—what's going on? Who was this man?"

"I'm not sure. But I'm going to find out."

"Why was he watching my apartment? What did he want?"

"I don't know, but it has to do with me, not you, okay?"

She hurried off into the bedroom, then came back a moment later with her cell phone.

"Who are you calling?" I asked.

"The police, who the hell do you think?"

"Don't."

"Are you out of your mind? There was someone watching my apartment in the middle of the night and you expect me—"

"Put the phone down, Sophie." I joined her in the kitchenette. "Please."

She kept the phone in her hand but let it drop down to her side with a dramatic sigh. "I don't—you need to explain to me what's happening, okay?"

She looked like she might burst into tears at any moment. "I don't—I mean—I'm half-asleep and now I'm scared out of my mind, there was a man *watching* us?"

"It's all right, it—"

"No, it's not all right!"

"You can't call the cops, Soph."

"Oh, I can't? Why, because I don't have your permission?"

"It's not like that."

"Well, by all means, Stan, tell me what it's like then." She folded her arms across her chest. "Please, fill me in."

"I told you it wasn't a good idea for us to get involved or for me to come here, remember? Whoever this guy is, it's me he's interested in, not you."

"But who is he?"

"I don't know yet. But he had one of those cards, Soph, like the blank one I was telling you about I found."

"What is it? What is it for, what does it mean?"

"I don't know."

"But he's involved with what happened to you?"

"Yes."

"And he knows where I live. Where I *live*! I—I can't stay here. He could come back anytime and do God-knows-what to me!"

"You can stay at my place if you want, but—"

"Great, I'm sure that's a completely safe hideout. He'll never find us there."

"We won't need a hideout. I just want you to feel safe, okay?"

"*Safe*?" she said through a rapid-fire burst of nervous laughter. "I'm calling the police."

"Sophie, please." I reached out for her but came just short of touching her. "*Please*. No cops."

She began pacing near the sink. "Why?"

I brought my hands to my head and ran them through my hair. "Something happened to me Thursday night. I don't know what, but it was more than me getting drunk and blacking out. There's more to it but I can't remember. No matter how hard I try, I can't. I think someone robbed me, convinced me somehow to give them all my money. Maybe it was this guy, I don't know, but he's connected to what happened, I'm sure of it. I just don't know how or why. What I *do* know is this has nothing to do with you. He was watching your apartment because I was in it."

"And if you hadn't seen him in time, he would've—what—broken in?"

"I should've never come here. I'm sorry."

"But you did." She grabbed her cigarettes and lit one. "I invited you, I wanted you to come, I just didn't realize…"

"I know," I said softly.

"I'm connected to it now because I'm connected to you. I'm part of it."

"No, you're not. I'll handle this."

"I don't understand why we can't call the police and let them deal with this."

"They can't help me, and they can't protect us. If you bring them into this, it'll make things worse, trust me." She looked thoroughly unconvinced, so I continued. "I used to swim in the same cesspool the guy I ran into out there tonight does now, do you understand? I know how things work on the street. No cops."

She puffed her cigarette. "Okay, fine—what—whatever."

"If you don't want to stay here, you can come to my place," I said. "If you're not comfortable with that, maybe you could crash at your son's for a while?"

"He lives in the western part of the state. It's like three hours from here."

"Maybe getting out of the area for a few days is a good idea."

"Stan, I have to work Monday. So do you."

Balthazar came slinking out of the bedroom, squinting at us through a giant yawn. He stretched and arched his back, then found his way over to Sophie, winding around and between her ankles in a serpentine motion. Leaving the cigarette in her mouth, Sophie scooped him up and held him close.

"I'm not going to leave you here if you don't feel safe."

Holding her cigarette in one hand and her cat in the other, Sophie asked, "Then what do we do?"

"Pack some things and you can stay at my place for a while," I said. "I know it's not ideal but what other options are there?"

She finished her cigarette, then tossed it in the sink and ran the water until the butt was extinguished. "What about Balthazar?" she asked, nuzzling him. "I'm not going without him."

"Pack up his food and toys and litter box and bring him with us."

"Really?"

"Of course."

"Thanks." A slight smile appeared, then vanished. "It's not like we're your responsibility or anything."

"Call it looking out for each other, okay?"

"Okay."

"I'm so sorry I got you involved in all this, Soph. I never meant for things to go like this or—"

"It's not your fault."

"Yes it is."

"I'm a grown woman. You warned me. I made my choice."

I wanted to put my arms around her but stayed where I was, just out of reach. "I'm going to get this worked out."

She put Balthazar down on the counter. "I'll pack some things."

I looked over at the vase on the floor, the flowers scattered about and the puddle of water, but the only pictures in my head were the nightmares haunting the dark recesses of my mind. And wrapped in shadow, visions of Chic's rat eyes staring at me, damning us both for things I couldn't yet understand.

Crouching down, I picked up one of the flowers. Drawn to it for some reason, I stared at it a while, trying to make sense of things, but couldn't remember anything more.

Balthazar watched me from his perch on the counter as I snapped a good portion of the stem from the flower. I decided to present it to Sophie when she came back out of the bedroom with her things. It's all I had. The night was dying, but still, there was beauty. Damaged and dying itself, but beauty nonetheless, a tiny bit of hope, floating alone in a sea of deepening madness.

Despite the odd power of that, it was the wasted years, bad dreams and darkness running through my veins like the poisons they were that took hold and throttled me. Maybe all my sins had finally come home to roost, or maybe I was a superstitious fool afraid of my own shadow and the things hidden within it. Didn't much matter either way.

There'd be no escaping any of this.

11

BACK AT MY PLACE, once I'd finally gotten Sophie settled in and calmed down, we both lay down with Balthazar in the quiet of my bedroom. We didn't speak. We just lay there for a long while, my arms around her and my fingers gently stroking her forehead until she finally drifted off to sleep. I'd forgotten what it was like to be so physically close like that. I missed it. Still, I knew it would be short-lived, at least for now. This was not the time for hearts and flowers. It was all blood and barbed wire now.

The cat, still spooked by new surroundings, stayed close to Sophie, snuggled up under the covers and peering out at me as if for assurance everything would be all right. With great care, I managed to wiggle free from Sophie without waking her. I gave Balthazar a reassuring pat on the head, then rolled out of bed and padded over to my closet. Sliding the lockbox down from the top shelf, I moved quietly as I could into the kitchen.

But for the soft whisper of fans, I sat in silence at the kitchen table. I poured myself a whiskey, then opened the combination lock on the box, set it aside and had a long drink. The liquor moved through me, warm and soothing. After staring at it for what seemed an eternity, I flipped open the box and removed everything but the police scanner, the sunglasses and the counterfeit licenses. Laying the other items out carefully on the table before me, I considered them all a moment.

Once I touched them, they'd become real.

Carefully, I chose the Kubotan first, holding it in my hand for a time before changing grips. A series of moves I'd learned years before returned to me, along with a flash of memory, reminding me of the last person I'd used the weapon on, a guy in a bar in Revere I'd had business with. I remembered using the Kubotan to bend his thumb back until it broke. I could still hear that awful sound—like the snap of a dry twig—all these years later. I returned the Kubotan to the box and next selected the brass knuckles. Heavier than I remembered, they came with their own memories, none pleasant. It was hard to admit I'd once been a person that used such things, but violence was never far, the ability to return to it if necessary closer than it seemed. I placed the brass knuckles back in the box, then turned my attention to the driving gloves. They were stiff and cracked. I set them aside and opened the cleaning kit. Everything I needed was there, so I took hold of the Beretta, inspected then set to cleaning it. Although I couldn't remember the last time I'd done it, within seconds I was deftly cleaning the weapon with as much expertise, precision and care as I had years ago.

Once satisfied, I loaded one of the clips, then laid the gun down on the table. It was ready to go, but did I really want to leave the house carrying a firearm? I'd promised myself I'd never do such a thing again, but I'd broken the rest of my promises over the years, what was one more? Besides, if I was going to find out what was going on, it needed to be done oldschool. This wasn't a game. Whatever I was dealing with was serious, and that meant I needed to be the same.

I penned a note to Sophie, telling her I'd gone out for a while, to stay put and that I'd be back soon. I hoped she'd sleep through the night. By the time I got back, maybe I'd know more and be closer to putting this behind us.

I locked the box and returned it to the closet shelf, ignoring the shotgun propped in the back corner. Returning to the kitchen, I left the note in plain view on the table. I seriously doubted I'd need an extra clip, so I hid it in a seldom-used drawer, then tucked the Beretta in my belt and pulled my shirt down over it.

Minutes later I was behind the wheel of my car, a plan still formulating in my mind, but it felt freeing to be outside and moving through the night again. Before leaving the area, I did a thorough inspection of the neighborhood to make sure there was no one watching from the shadows. Once satisfied, I took off. It was after three in the morning and everything was quiet, still and dark. I thought about Duane, down on the sand out there, dreaming of better days. I thought about my old man rotting in his own filth and sins, dreaming about Florida and an easier life he didn't deserve. I thought about Sophie and the fear in her eyes, asleep and unaware in my bed now. And me, with no dreams at all, adrenaline pumping as I glided through the dark like all those years before, looking for people who didn't want to be found and might not survive if they were. With neither rhyme nor reason, a man possessed, I drove, smothered by myriad emotions that slowly became a shroud of cold, predatory detachment. Just like the earlier warmth, I hadn't experienced that in a very long time. It was like being half-dead, but also familiar and comfortable, an old coat pulled from storage and slipped on like a second skin. Doing certain things with clarity and extreme prejudice required becoming less than wholly human, and I could already feel myself sliding down into that empty pit.

Avoiding the areas where cops congregated after dark, eventually I found myself leaving town and pulling onto the state highway. The green glow of the dashboard lights made things seem even more surreal and dreamlike, so I switched the radio on and let some tunes distract me a while.

I arrived in Brockton a little over half an hour later, and following the GPS on my phone, located Chic's address in a shitty neighborhood of aged duplexes and run-down apartment buildings. His was a boxy two-story building, but his van was nowhere in sight and both floors were dark. I found a spot at the top of the block, pulled over and parked. No other cars had passed since I'd arrived and none of the buildings on the street had any lights on, so I slouched down in the seat and waited, my eyes moving from the windshield to the left side mirror, to the rearview to the right side mirror then back again, covering every angle, watching the night.

More memories returned, forcing me back to places and times I wanted to keep buried in the murky depths of yesterdays-gone-wrong and bad dreams that came to me at the worst of times and left me drenched in sweat and mumbling lies. Monsters under my bed, clawing their way through my nightmares to remind me that they were still as real as anything else, because I'd never be able to kill them all. There were too many. I was outnumbered.

*　*　*

Night. Waves crashing. Smell of blood and piss and ocean in the air. Terror.

Cigarette smoke, cocaine and booze coming out of our pores—me, Johnny Fitz and Fenway Dave—my boys, all leather and denim, attitude and strut.

It's a violent night, but aren't they all?

Some guy named Pete or Paul or Randy or Frank, makes no difference, he's bloodied and staggering around and choking on his own tears and snot. Older than any of us, old enough to be our father, he's probably fifty, his pants stained and torn, shirttails blowing about in the wind, eyeglasses askew, one lens cracked.

Like me, Fenway Dave is mostly quiet, stands off to the side smoking a cigarette, more bored than bothered. Just another night in paradise, straightening out the fools who borrow and don't pay. How did I end up here? When did I become this person? I can't even remember. It just happened. Maybe I was always this guy and didn't know it. But even then, as Peter or Paul or Randy or Frank stumbles around in the thick sand, bleeding from his nose and freshly split lips, babbling about how sorry he is and that we don't need to do this, I only know I don't want to be here. I want to be anywhere but here. Anywhere. I just want it to stop. I want to be a little boy again, but this time without the pain. I want Johnny and Dave to finish what they have to finish so we can go get paid, grab some drinks, find some women and forget all this.

Peter or Paul or Randy or Frank knows we're not going to kill him. They only do that shit in the movies. A corpse can't pay the vig, and sharks are all about the vig. They pay you so you can pay them back more than they lent you. No different than the big Wall Street boys, really, just no one in our world pretends it's anything other than what it is: grimy and grotesque and horrible, the underbelly minefields of a world already gone mad. What Peter or Paul or Randy or Frank does know is that we're going to hurt him. The question is, how bad? Is it already over? A couple slaps and a punch or two from Johnny Fitz then go on and get out of our sight? Or will it be worse?

Johnny Fitz, all operatic and larger-than-life. Big mouth, big laugh, big violence. I've known him since we were in our early teens, and he's always been a menace. Looks like Fonzie on Happy Days, *only bigger and meaner.*

"Got to do the right thing," he says.

"Definitely," Peter or Paul or Randy or Frank says. "Tell him, I'll—"

"I'm not telling nobody shit. What am I, your fucking secretary?"

"No," he says, dropping to his knees, barely able to control his weeping. "No."

Johnny Fitz moves closer, lords over him, taking a quick second to glance back at me and Fenway Dave and smile. He's having a good time. For Dave and me this is all business. Johnny Fitz actually enjoys this shit. He positions himself over the guy like he's going to get a blowjob, reaches down, grabs a handful of his hair and yanks his head back so he's looking up at him. "Do the right thing. Handle it. If we have to come back and take you for another ride, it ain't gonna be to the sand, you hear me? You're going out there." He motions to the dark ocean. "Yeah?"

He nods, falls against the front of Johnny's thighs, crying. "Yes."

"Fuck off me," he snaps, pushing him away.

He falls into the sand on his back, still crying, probably from relief now. Until Johnny puts the boot to him, that is.

Then the cries become more urgent and violent as the pain gets worse and the horror of being beaten and humiliated nearly drowns him.

I look away; watch the street, the water, anything but this.

Fenway Dave flicks his cigarette away and casually walks over to them, steps in front of Johnny before he really does kill this guy. "Easy," Dave says in his typical quiet voice. "You ghost this idiot, we're all fucked."

Johnny Fitz nods, understands what he's saying. We're here to convince him it's in his best interest to pay his debt. Doesn't matter how, just get it done or more of this is coming your way. Johnny accidentally kills him and we'll not only graduate to murderers, we'll be on the line for the stupid bastard's debt. All that's going to do is bring huge amounts of heat on us, our boss and his bosses, and nobody wants that. Johnny Fitz points at Peter or Paul or Randy or Frank. "Do the right thing, you piece of shit. You make us come back, we'll be the last thing you ever see."

Fenway Dave guides Johnny away, careful not to be too forceful about it. He's saving the other guy's ass, not telling Johnny what to do. There's a pecking order and it needs to be respected. As they pass by, Dave cocks his head toward the guy, who still lies flat on his back, blubbering. I nod.

As they head for the car, I walk over to the guy and crouch down next to him in the sand. "He's not playing with you," I tell him. "You understand?"

"Yes," he gasps, raising his hands. "Please...don't..."

He's so sad, this guy. Lying there like some little kid knocked down and beat up on a playground. Only he's a grown man with a family at home, a wife and kids who look up to him, who love and respect him. And I'm a punk. But I don't make the rules. Nobody ever said you have to like those rules, but if you want to stay on the still-alive side of things, you do have to follow them. I'm the cleanup guy, the last bullpen call at the end of the game, here to throw the last few pitches and close shit out. That's how we do it. Fenway Dave's the starter. His smooth talk readies them for what's coming. Johnny Fitz comes in for middle relief and softens them up, let's them understand they can't win. And I'm the closer. Like when we steal, they handle the robbing, I do the driving. Everybody's got a job to do, and they're all bad because we're swimming in shit. There are no good days.

"Make sure you give them a call before tomorrow night," I tell the poor bastard.

He nods, whimpers like a child. I don't know who this guy is and I can't care about that right now. But I do know he's not like us. Guy's probably a shoe salesman or a mailman or something, a regular guy who hit a bad time or maybe has a weakness for gambling or other things, a guy with bad credit who has to sneak around to places he shouldn't go so he can get some quick cash. There are people at home he'll have to make excuses and lie to about his injuries. He fell, or he was mugged or who knows what else. I know them all. My mother knew them all. They're all the same, always the same.

He doesn't belong here, this guy, on this dark beach with animals like us. But here he is. Here we all are.

I drop an elbow on him. Hard. Breaks his glasses in two and splits the skin just above his left eye. He cries out and brings his hands to the wound, but it's already spurting blood all over the place. I stand in time to miss most of it, but a bit sprays across the front of my jeans.

"Please," he cries. "No more—please—I-I'll take care of it, I promise, I..."

I nod, even though he can't see me through the blood and darkness. A part of me sees myself—sometimes even my mother—when I look at these slobs, and I wonder why I don't help them. Shouldn't I know better? Shouldn't I be the guy that doesn't hurt people? I don't want to, never felt good about it, but I'm to a point where I don't feel anything, and maybe that's the problem. Like when my old man pounded away on me, eventually I didn't feel a goddamn thing. Hunter or hunted, makes no difference.

Back on the ridge overlooking the beach, Johnny Fitz and Fenway Dave stand watching me, waiting. There's more drugs to do, more drinks to be had, plenty of forgetting and numbing to do. In a few years they'll both be dead. Dave dies in the street before an ambulance can get to him, gunned down outside a bar by the husband of some woman he was running around with. A year later Johnny gets sent to Walpole for a double murder he and another guy pull while robbing an underground casino in Chinatown. He dies in prison a month later when another inmate shanks him in the shower, cashing in on the contract the Chinese mob put out on him for raiding their game and killing two of their own.

And me? I think I escape, swear I've found salvation—and maybe I do—only to have it ripped from my grasp with as little mercy as I show this poor fuck and the rest we deal with. Never killed anyone. Came close but stopped just short, and at the point where it was either move through those gates or go the other way, I made what most would say was the right move.

Doesn't matter where I go or even who I am from there, though. Those old ghosts never die. Can't kill what's already dead. I feel them moving under my skin and always will, gnawing at my bones like the ravenous cannibals they are. It's all inside me, a bad dream I never wake up from.

So I go blind instead.

The past fades to black, where it belongs.

* * *

I don't know how long I sat out there, but eventually a pair of headlights cut the night and turned at the top of the street. They were followed by a second. The first was Chic's van, the second a dark sedan. The van pulled into the space in front of his address, the second stopped in the middle of the street. The van's driver-side door opened and a man got out. It wasn't Chic but some other guy I couldn't make out in the dark. He walked over to the sedan and got in the back just as the front side door of the car opened and a dark form tumbled out and rolled to the curb.

Even before the person regained his feet and revealed himself to be Chic, the door was pulled closed and the car sped off, passing by me and turning the corner at the end of the block before vanishing into darkness.

In my rearview, I saw Chic start up a side staircase toward his apartment.

He wasn't paying much attention to his surroundings, probably still caught up in whatever had happened to him earlier, none of which could've been good, so I hopped out of the car and hurried along the sidewalk until I was directly across from his building. By the time I got there he was halfway up the staircase and headed for the door to the third-floor apartment.

There was no way to ascend the rickety wooden staircase quietly, so with a deep breath, I grabbed the railing and charged up the stairs as fast as I could.

I was still quite a distance from him when Chic heard me coming. It was dark and he hadn't left an outside light on so I couldn't see him that well and knew he couldn't make me out either.

As he fumbled with his keys in an attempt to get inside, I pushed myself up those stairs until I'd reached him. Chic had the keys in the door and had just started to push his way in when I closed on him, slamming into him from behind with such force we both stumbled inside. He lost his balance and nearly fell, catching himself at the last moment on the edge of a counter. I closed the door behind us, and just as he spun around, I pulled the gun and leveled it at him. There was enough moonlight through the windows over the nearby sink to reveal what I was pointing at him.

"Fuck is this?" he said, breathing heavy, hands raised.

"Turn a light on," I said, equally out of breath.

Chic reached for a wall switch, and suddenly a modest kitchen appeared around us. His face fell when he recognized me. "Fuck, man, not you."

"Afraid so, Chic." I motioned with the gun. "Weapons on the counter."

"I ain't packin'," he said.

I didn't trust anyone wearing a jacket in this heat, even a lightweight Members Only deal like he had on and I hadn't seen in years. "Lose the jacket."

Chic shook his head and carefully removed his jacket, peeling it back with one hand to his shoulders, then shaking it off until it fell to the floor, wincing throughout. When his other hand came into view, I realized why. He'd wrapped it haphazardly with what looked like a strip of fabric torn from perhaps a T-shirt, but the odd angles of his first three fingers left no doubt that they'd been broken, likely snapped one at a time.

"We alone, or is there a Mrs. Chic?"

"Just you and me, sweet pea."

"Have an accident?" I asked.

"Eat shit."

"You should go to the hospital."

"Fuck off, ace."

"Who did that to you?"

"Why don't you get the fuck out of my house? How about that?"

"Why'd they break your fingers, Chic?"

He looked like he might burst into tears. His fear was that raw. "You're gonna get me killed, boss. You're gonna get us both killed. That what you want?"

"What I want is information. And you're going to give it to me."

"I got neighbors. I make enough noise, they'll call the fuzzy bears."

"You're not going to make any noise, Chic."

"No?"

"No." I lowered the gun, and with my free hand pulled out one of the two chairs at the kitchen table. "Sit down."

He fidgeted about. "I don't—I don't want to sit down."

I stared at him. Whatever fight he may have had in him had already been beaten out of him, and we both knew it.

Chic slowly sank down into the chair, holding his damaged hand by the wrist. The broken fingers were still trembling occasionally. He wouldn't look at me, and I couldn't blame him.

"You've already had a bad night," I told him. "Doesn't have to get worse, but that's up to you, understand?"

He nodded.

I snagged a dishtowel hanging from the oven handle and threw it at him.

"Come on, chief," he said through nervous laughter. "I—I didn't even get a chance to answer anything yet, I—what do you—"

"You know the routine," I said.

He looked at me with such fear and pleading in his eyes I almost forgot the whole thing and left. I didn't want to hurt him, but I had to.

"Please," he said in an uncharacteristically soft voice. "I'll tell you anything you want to know, I—what I'm saying is, I—I'll cooperate, okay?"

"I know you will," I said sadly.

There was no way out, and he realized that now. He'd been through this kind of thing before. Better to get it over with soon as he could and hope for the best. I pointed to the table and his face twisted into a grimace. With his good hand, Chic stuffed the towel into his mouth, then slammed shut his eyes.

I wasn't sure I still had the stomach for such things, but I had to establish pain first. There was no other way to do it. You introduced pain as a way of letting him know what was waiting for him whenever he didn't cooperate. The threat was one thing, but there was no substitute for getting an actual taste of it.

You begin there and hope that's where it ends.

Chic put his mangled hand on the table.

I flipped the pistol around like a hammer, handle down, and slammed it onto his broken fingers. His cries were muffled by the towel, as was the whimpering that followed. His body rocked and shook a moment, head down, chest heaving, and then slowly, he became still and raised his head. His face was bright red, eyes brimming with tears and his hand shaking violently but still held in place on the table.

I nodded, granting him permission to remove his hand.

With another whimper, he let his hand slide back into his lap. I pulled the towel from his mouth and tossed it on the table. "Who broke your fingers?"

"Same people you trying to get to."

"Why?"

"Fucked up when I tailed you." He hung his head. "Wasn't supposed to get caught. They didn't want to be known…yet."

"Do you know what happened to me Thursday night?"

"Yeah, but I'm fringe, man, I—I ain't nobody, you dig?"

"Who are you? Who are these people?"

Chic's bloodshot eyes darted to the door as if he expected them to come bursting through it at any second. "Nobody you want to know."

"Why can't I remember you or the others? Why don't I remember going to the ATM and emptying my account?"

The way he looked at me, I'd have sworn that at that moment *he* felt sorry for *me*. "You think this is about a fucking *robbery*?" he asked in a loud whisper. "You got no idea what's happening."

"Answer me," I said. "Why don't I remember?"

"Because with *him* anything is possible."

"Who?"

Chic was consumed with such sorrow it stopped me dead. "The Devil."

12

DESPITE THE STIFLING HEAT in the apartment, a shiver spider-walked up my spine. "You're gonna have to do better than that, Chic."

"They brought him to you, let him breathe all over you."

"No riddles."

Chic dripped sweat and looked even more unhealthy and pasty in the wash of fluorescent kitchen light. "They'll kill me," he said. "Kill me, you dig?"

"You gonna make me hurt you again?"

He shook his head, licked his lips and looked down at the floor. "You don't understand what you're dealing with, boss."

"Neither do you."

"You think my life means anything to them? You think yours does?"

"Nobody needs to know I was even here, Chic."

"They'll know."

"How?"

"They're the wind. Everywhere. Nowhere."

I pulled the other chair out from the table, set it across from him and sat down, gun still in hand. "So what are these people, some sort of Devil freaks or something? A cult, what?"

"Ain't that simple." Chic moved like a caged animal, twitching and trembling, but he remained seated. "They're a part of something dark as shit, but—but it's not like that."

"What's it like then?"

He sighed. It was a sigh of defeat and submission. "It okay if I have a butt?"

"You can have a smoke when we're done."

"I know, I could use it as a weapon, right? I won't. You got my word, chief. I just really need a cigarette. Please, man."

I stood, retrieved his jacket from the floor and rummaged through the pockets until I found a pack of Lucky Strikes and a Zippo. I dropped the jacket back to the floor, selected a cigarette from the pack and stuck one in his mouth. After tossing the pack on the table, I flipped open the Zippo and held the flame for him as he inhaled and got the cigarette going.

"Thanks," he said quietly, the cigarette held between his lips.

I snapped shut the lighter, placed it on the table next to the cigarettes and sat down, facing him again. "Talk."

"Ever heard of the Borrachero tree?"

"No."

"It only grows in Colombia," Chic explained. "Has a plant on it called *brugmansia*. They call it The Devil's Breath 'cause it makes something called Scopolamine. It's a drug. It's legit all over the world, they use it to treat Parkinson's disease and shit like that. Thing is, see, in a raw form it turns people into fucking zombies. They take the flowers or leaves of the Borrechero tree and boil them, and then once they're liquefied, they can slip it into somebody's drink or put it in their food, dig? They grind it into a powder too. You blow that shit in somebody's face, it's instant personal zombie time." He puffed his cigarette, exhaled through his nose. "Game over, baby."

As I turn, a face explodes from the darkness and lunges for me...

"What do you mean by *zombie?*"

A demon—a witch—blows into its open palm...

"The Devil's Breath, chief."

Disperses a cloud of mist that sprays my face...

"Wipes away free will," Chic continued. "You do anything they tell you to do. No arguments, no resistance. Whatever they say, you do."

"How is that possible?"

"I don't know how or why it works, but it does. Sounds like bullshit, I get it, only it's not. They been using it in Colombia for years to rob people, rape chicks, whatever. Mostly used by scumbag street shit, even hookers use it down there on johns to get them to empty their bank accounts or run up their credit cards. And the best part is you wake up the next day with a giant hangover but don't remember shit. Just pieces, and that's if you're lucky."

"And these people, they have access to this drug and used it on me?"

"Yeah, but..."

"But what?"

"The Devil's Breath they got ain't like the shit down in Colombia, brother." Chic took another pull on his cigarette, still leaving it in his mouth. "You hear what I just told you? You think something that powerful, something that can do that kind of shit to people is gonna stay a drug for street thugs down in South America forever? Fucking military and government types got ahold of it. But some private groups did too. Financed by the elite, they did their work on it in labs, came up with something even better. A stronger version, part original drug and part synthetic, dig it? This one's worse than the original, more powerful. It wipes the memory clean in almost every victim. It's better than the original, 'cause with the original, now and then the memory loss wears off, right? But with this new breed it stays gone in almost everybody. It breaks down the resistance even longer. Total control, boss, *total* control, you see?"

I stood up and pushed my chair back to the table. I needed to move. I needed fresh air, needed to clear my head. "And these people have this stronger version?"

Chic nodded, reached up with his good hand and plucked what was left of the cigarette from his mouth. "You got to be careful how you use it. Shit can be lethal if you don't know what you're doing. A gram of the original stuff can kill up to fifteen people, man, and that's some serious shit. Same amount of the new strain can ice twice that many. That's the stuff they used on you, bro."

"Why?" I asked.

"You were chosen."

"Chosen? Chosen for what, why me?"

"I don't know, man. I'm nobody, baby, you got to understand that."

I thought a moment, letting it all sink in as I tried to make sense of the vague traces of memory I had about that night. They weren't dreams or strange visions after all. It really had happened. They'd blown this drug in my face and I'd inhaled it, gotten it in my eyes and mouth, where it was absorbed into my bloodstream and turned me into a slave to their every whim.

"When they were done with you, they dumped you back on the street and told you to go home. And like a good little zombie, you did. Best part is people on it don't act like they're drugged. They seem normal. Maybe a little relaxed but still them, dig it? Look like them, sound like them, the whole nut. Understand now why you can't remember nothing and had the worst hangover of your life the next morning, big daddy?"

"So they hit me with this shit on my way home from work," I said. "Then they take me to the ATM and tell me to empty my bank account..."

"Devil was breathing all over you, baby."

"But it's not about robbery," I reminded him. "That's what you said."

Chic nodded.

"What then?"

"Ones behind the curtain, the wizards, they don't care about your money."

"And who are the wizards?"

Chic raised his cigarette. It was almost gone. "Need to put this out, boss."

I motioned to a plastic ashtray on the table. He leaned forward and crushed the butt, then sat back, holding his bad hand by the wrist again.

"Who are they?" I asked again.

Chic was nervous and not hiding it well. "It ain't that easy."

"Why not?"

"Because it ain't, brother man, I—you got to understand, it's—this isn't like some little group of losers fucking with people. It goes a lot deeper than that, it's—it's bigger, you dig? It's bigger than either of us knows."

"Fine," I said, "then let's start with who you work for."

"I don't work for nobody. I'm a free agent."

"Who hired you to tail me?"

"It's not about hiring. It's a debt owed. It's about blood."

"You're testing my patience, Chic, and you're making me very angry."

"No, no, hold up, hold up. I ain't nobody, dig? I'm way down, boss, strictly minor leagues. I hang around, I try to learn, but I'm not even really in with them, not—not yet."

"In with who?"

He didn't answer. Keeping the gun down by my leg, I backhanded him across the mouth with my other hand. Quickly. Savagely. Chic's head snapped back, and he let out a groan, but he stayed seated and clutching his wrist.

A few seconds came and went, and still no answer, so I hit him again.

Blood trickled from his nose, ringing his mouth and ending in a slow drip from his chin. "Okay," he said, his speech slurred from the split bottom lip the first blow had caused. "Stop, I...okay..."

"Next time I'll pull those broken fingers clean out of their sockets, got it?"

"Chill, baby, I—I'm receiving you loud and clear, okay? I'm your guy."

I stared at him but he knew I wouldn't ask a third time. Even if I did, he'd be in so much pain he wouldn't hear me anyway.

"The Brotherhood," he said softly, shaking his head in despair, as if by simply uttering the words all was lost. "It's big, the real people involved. I—I don't know that much about that part yet, I—I only just started hanging around in a few circles a while back, dig? I hang out and I hear things, right? But I'm so low even the ones doing the scut work give me orders, bro. I ain't nothing."

"How'd you get involved with these people in the first place?"

"Knew some motherfuckers who knew some motherfuckers. Figured maybe I could make some bread, you know? I'm on the grift like everybody else, chief, just hustling and bustling, trying to make my way." Blood was still leaking from his nose. He pawed the blood from his face and mouth with his good hand, then wiped his hand on his shirt. "I heard some things and—"

"What kind of things?"

"Like some of the people I was running with were low-level dudes that did dirty work for bigger fish, more important money guys into some crazy dark religious shit. Rich, powerful motherfuckers, the ones that run everything, you know. The *elite*." He wiped more blood from his nose. "Can I get a fucking tissue?"

"Sounds like a bunch of conspiracy-theory bullshit to me," I said, tossing him the dishtowel.

"I know, right?" He pushed the towel up under his nose and let his mangled hand rest against the side of the table. "Bunch of rich fucks playing gods, running shit and pulling the strings behind the scenes, having people like me and the rest run shit from the street up. Got to control the sheep, see?"

"Where do I find these people?" I asked.

"They find you."

"How about your contacts, these thugs running shit from the street up?"

He looked at me, hopelessness in his eyes. "Come on, man."

I tapped the gun gently against the outside of my thigh and stepped closer.

"Okay, wait! I—I hang out at this club in Sunset, little dive called The Cube."

"Never heard of it."

"It's over by the dunes, on the other side of town from the drag, bro."

"Go on."

"They're minor league too, small potatoes, okay? They—we—we're all low-level frontline guys. But they're bigger than me, in deeper than me, dig?"

"I need a name, Chic."

He closed his eyes. "Felix."

"Like the cat?"

"He ain't shit either. But at that level, he's the man."

"Is he the one who drugged me?"

"I don't know. I wasn't there, man."

I watched him a while but couldn't be sure if he was telling the whole truth. Probably, because every time he lied it was obvious, but he might've been bluffing. Even a lousy liar like Chic pulled one off now and then.

"You lying to me?"

"Would I do that now that we're such good friends and all?"

"What else did they do to me?" I asked. "Where did they take me that night?"

"I swear to God, I don't know."

I turned the gun around like a hammer again.

"For real, for real! I swear on my mother's grave, bro, I don't know!"

I hesitated.

"They just told me to follow you," he said. "That's it. I don't even know who the fuck you are, all right? For real."

I removed his driver's license along with the black business card I'd taken from him and placed them both on his kitchen table. I left the other card in my wallet. "What does the black card mean?"

"It's a way in," he said.

"A way in where?"

"Everything. Just depends how high up you are."

"How'd I end up with one?"

"Couldn't tell you even if I wanted to, chief."

"Guess."

He winced, maybe from pain, maybe from my question. Maybe both. "Safe bet somebody fucked up the night they had you, left one around and you snagged it. You probably didn't know you did. Or maybe you had one of them—what they call it—*moments of clarity*, right? Maybe you had one of them and grabbed it thinking it'd help you remember what happened."

"Do they know I have it?"

"What do you think?"

"Was that part of what you were supposed to do, get it back?"

He nodded.

"So this gets me into what, the club, The Cube?"

"Some of them do. Depends on the level. All them cards got barcodes on them you can't see. Some get you into a place like The Cube. Some get you into bigger things, like meetings or even the big nights. All depends on your level, dig?"

"What are these *big nights*?"

"The ritual nights, I—I don't know nothing about them. Some say they ain't even real, that it's all bullshit and talk, but Felix said he seen one once. Maybe he's lying, maybe not, I got no idea. It's all talk, brother, all whispers and rumors, you know? Big secret meetings where they supposedly do all this dark shit behind closed doors, but who knows for sure? Ones who do ain't talking, dig?"

A siren down the street interrupted the silence, then faded into the distance.

"Tell me about The Brotherhood," I said.

"Brotherhood of Saturn," he answered in a loud whisper. "That's what they call themselves."

"Why? What's the point?"

"I don't know." He looked away. "Ask them."

"Come on, Chic, you were doing so well."

"I don't want to die," he said quietly.

"I'm not going to kill you."

"I know. Gonna die anyways though."

"Not if—"

"Don't matter. I'm already dead, boss." Chic looked up at me, bloody and teary-eyed. "And you probably are too. Like I said, you got no idea what you're dealing with."

"What, a bunch of punks who use some exotic drug to rob people when they're not hanging out at a shithole club and telling spooky stories to morons like you who listen to their bullshit? Seriously?"

"It ain't them. Ain't what you see, dig? Just like the world, daddy, don't have to worry about the one that's out front. It's the other one, the one *behind* it you got to worry about." He checked the towel, his nose was still bleeding so he put it back up under his nostrils and held it there. "Hidden things are hidden for a reason. They want to stay that way. Even when they hide in plain sight, like most of them do."

He was scared to death, and it was obvious he considered me to be the least of his problems.

"You killed me the minute you walked through that door, boss." He inspected the towel again, then put it on the table, apparently satisfied his nose had stopped or sufficiently slowed its bleeding.

For the first time, I allowed myself to focus on something other than Chic. His apartment was small and cramped, unkempt and cluttered. The stove was filthy, the sink full of dishes. "How long do the effects of The Devil's Breath last?"

"Hours. But with this new stronger strain, who knows?"

"What about side effects or flashbacks, that kind of thing?"

"Ain't no doctor or scientist, man, how am I supposed to know?"

I tightened my grip on the gun because I didn't want Chic to see my hand shaking. "Something more happened to me that night, I…I have these horrible dreams."

"They're not dreams, baby."

"What did they do to me?"

"I swear I don't know."

I believed him.

"I've been straight with you. Can you do me a solid? In that cupboard." He pointed to a cabinet above the sink. "Behind the big bowl, grab that for me."

Keeping an eye on him, I opened the cupboard, reached behind a large plastic bowl and came back with a prescription bottle of pills. There was no label and it only contained two pills. "What are they?" I asked.

"Oxy." He held up his mangled hand. "This really fucking hurts, bro."

I opened the bottle and tapped it until both pills fell into his open hand.

"There's a couple beers in the fridge," he said. "Take one for you too, if you want, fuck it."

In the refrigerator I found four cans of cheap beer, the remains of a sandwich and a small container of milk, long soured. I grabbed a beer, opened it and put it on the table for him.

"Thanks."

"Pleasure or pain," I told him. "Up to you."

Chic took a long swallow of beer. "God damn," he said, fondly looking at the can. "Nothing like a cold beer, is there? One of the best things in the world."

I glanced around a bit more. In Chic's lonely and dark world, a cold beer was likely one of the few bright spots. His walls were covered with nude centerfolds and bikini-clad women stretched out seductively across hotrods and motorcycles. The furniture, what little there was of it, was cheap and worn, and the entire place was shrouded with a feeling of sorrow and loneliness.

"Like I told you," Chic explained, "they supposedly have these *meetings*. I've never been to one but I heard about them. Word is they do things, fucked up things. Rituals. I don't know how much is true. Like you said, people talk a lot of shit, you know, so who knows? But whatever they're up to, it's nothing good. They pray to the dark, my man."

"The dark?"

"Saturn."

"The planet?"

"The god."

On the wall, a crude painting of an old man lords over me. Even in the limited light, I see he is sitting on a throne of sorts. His hair is long and unruly, as is his beard.

"They worship the planet too," he said. "It's all connected, dig?"

In his hand he holds a scythe…

"Connected to what?" I asked.

And he is surrounded by numerous symbols written in blood that look similar to the letter T…

"I don't know. Like I said, still being brought in slow. Or at least I was. Don't matter now. Nothing does." Chic gave a sad little shrug. "Never really did, I guess."

"Where do they hold these meetings?"

"Not sure, but I heard they use a lot of different places so it's harder to track them or know where they're gonna be. A lot of them don't even know until right before they do it."

"They do this kind of thing a lot?"

"More than you'd think."

"So what's the move, Chic? Walk away and hope for the best?"

"Put that gun in your mouth and pull the trigger."

Memories of the razor nearing my wrist closed on me. My stomach churned so violently I thought I might be sick. I feigned indifference but could tell Chic had sensed something, a hint in my expression perhaps. "Over these fools?" I gave a mock chuckle. "Unlikely."

"Got to slam these." He looked at the pills in his hand. "Pain's too much."

"Hold off until we're done, I need you coherent."

He nodded. "I didn't even do nothing, and here I am talking to you with my hand all fucked up and you beating on me like I'm a fucking speed bag."

Flashes of someone else—a woman—blinked across my mind's eye, gone before I could get a handle on them. "I need to know what happened that night."

"Can't help you with that, doggie dog." He smiled, his teeth stained with gold and blood. "Nobody can."

"You know where I can find Felix, besides The Cube?"

"Nah. He's either there or he's not."

"Get over to the hospital," I said, "have them fix up those fingers."

With a heavy sigh, he popped the pills into his mouth. "None of that matters."

Seemed at that point like I'd gotten whatever pertinent information he had. "Stay out of my way and we won't have any more problems."

"Sure thing, daddy." He winked. "Not sure where I'm going, but I'll see you when I see you, dig?"

I had no idea what he was talking about, until he began to cough, choke, then convulse. He was clearly having trouble breathing, and the smug look he'd had just seconds earlier became one of panic and agony.

"What is it?" I said.

The beer can dropped to the floor, fizzed and rolled away under the table as Chic's eyes rolled to white and his body toppled from the chair.

"Christ, what the fuck?" I backed away, stunned and confused.

His body was suddenly gripped by a series of horrific seizures.

The pills. Christ Jesus, the *pills.*

Writhing around on the floor, he gagged as gurgling noises emanated from his throat, and then another violent seizure hit him and his body, though stiff, went still.

By the time I realized he'd likely ingested cyanide rather than the Oxycodone he'd claimed they were, Chic was dead. I crouched down, hesitant to touch him. For some reason, I muttered his name, still in shock and unable to believe he'd killed himself right in front of me.

Who the hell keeps cyanide pills in his cupboard? I'd never seen anyone do such a thing outside of a spy novel or a movie.

Guilt fell across me like a shroud. I stood and ran my hands through my hair.

Poor bastard, I thought. The finality of it all—the tragedy of it—hit me like a hammer, and I wondered how I'd been so close to such a thing myself just days ago. From this perspective it seemed so different, unreasonable and reckless, and yet I understood that kind of fear and surrender better than most.

Horrified, I asked whatever might be listening for absolution.

Panic answered. There was a dead man that had clearly been beaten and tortured and here I was in his apartment in the middle of the night with an unregistered firearm and his blood on my knuckles. I grabbed the dishtowel and began wiping down everything I could remember touching since I'd gotten there.

I'd missed it, but now I knew Chic had been as trapped as I was. Only the demons had changed, and in the end, he'd been so frightened of these people that taking his own life was preferable to dealing with them again.

They pray to the dark.

Tucking the 9mm in my belt, I headed back out into the night, well aware that the darkness was no longer mine.

It belonged to them.

13

DOWN ON THE STREET, I could see the earliest hints of daylight breaking over the distant cityscape. Just barely on the right side of full-tilt panic, despite the heat and dripping sweat, I felt remarkably cold. An awful wave of paranoia latched on, strangling me with the steady, increasingly violent precision of a giant snake, its body slinking and swirling in the slowly morphing darkness with a beauty and finesse that seemed in direct conflict with its intentions. I wanted—needed—to feel alone just then, but didn't. In fact, I felt anything but. Certain I was being watched, at my car I stopped and searched the dark street, looking in one direction, and then the next. Nothing. No one.

A toppled metal trash can sounded from a nearby alley, the clang echoing along the empty street and ringing in the darkness. I looked toward the alley, saw something small and dark scurry off into the shadows.

A cat, I thought, *just some stray cat or—or maybe a large rat.*

I remained perfectly still, kept my breathing shallow, and listened.

In the distance, perhaps at the far end of that same alley, I heard what sounded like footfalls. Slow. Steady. Coming closer.

Staring at the mouth of the alley, I waited.

Something separated from the night to form the vague silhouette of a man standing there. The flare of a match hissed as he lit a cigarette, and for the briefest moment it revealed a jawline and the side of a man's face. But before I could make out any detail, the flame was extinguished and a veil of gray smoke spiraled off into darkness.

From behind me came a soft suggestion of grotesque, backward prayers.

At the far end of the block stood a second silhouette, watching me from the corner. After a moment, it was joined by a third, and then a fourth. I looked back at the alley. Two others had joined the smoking man as well.

I jumped into the car, turned the ignition and pulled out, quickly but careful not to squeal the tires, as I didn't want any potential witnesses seeing my car leaving the area. But once I got moving, I floored it.

The men at the mouth of the alley stepped back into darkness as I passed, and when I checked my rearview, just before turning at the top of the block, I saw the others had slipped back into hiding as well.

This is crazy, I thought. *How the hell did they find me so quickly? How could they have possibly known I was here?*

I made it to the highway without incident, so I dropped the window and let the warm air wash over me. My heart rate was back under control but I was still perspiring buckets and wired with nervous energy that was positively electric. There weren't many cars on the road at this hour, but I kept an eye on all my mirrors nonetheless, watching to see if anyone was following me.

By the time I took the exit for Sunset, I was convinced no one was tailing me, as once off the highway, there was virtually no traffic and it was much easier to spot a tail. Still, to be sure, I took the longest possible route to my house.

The sun was rising over the ocean, a new day burning its way through the darkness. I drove up to my cottage tentatively, hopeful Sophie was still asleep and not even aware I was gone. The house was dark, so I got out of the car and walked over to the path overlooking the beach. I couldn't seem to get hold of a single thought long enough to make much sense of anything, so rather than go inside, I followed the path across the bluff, onto the dunes and down to the beach.

Once there, I stood near the waterline, watching the gentle waves lap shore and the wet sand at my feet. The distant sky was already dominated by the brilliant orange glow of the rising sun, and despite everything, for just a few seconds, I felt a bit of peace. Even in the darkest moments, beauty appeared.

"Hey, man, what are you doing down here so early?"

I spun around, one hand instinctively reaching for the gun.

Duane smiled with his brown teeth and scratched at his head, his fingers disappearing in the tangle of dirty hair. He looked as if he'd just woken up, which he likely had. "Chill," he muttered. "It's just me."

"Didn't see you there," I said, relaxing as much as I was capable. Back in the day, no one could've gotten that close to me without my knowing they were there. And although I was glad it was only Duane standing behind me, his presence forced me to realize I needed to sharpen my senses, get back on the clock, and stay there. "Need to sort some shit out. Thought I'd watch the sun come up a while."

Duane pulled his rags-for-clothes in tighter around him. The temperature had dropped a bit but it was still hot, too hot for all the layers he had on. "Beautiful, huh?"

"You'd think living here I'd be more aware of just how beautiful it is."

"I see it come up every morning, watch it go down every night." He shrugged. "But, you know, I live outside, so, sort of makes sense that I would, I guess."

I felt myself smile. Had to love Duane.

"You need some alone time?" he asked.

I'd seen a man killed once before, and though it had been years ago, it still haunted me. That time I was a bystander, and while I could've done something to stop it, doing so would've put my own life at risk, as well as the lives of those with me. This time was different. Chic took his own life right in front of me, and directly because I'd cornered him and made him choose between dealing with me or with those out there in the dark. Now he was dead, and just as surely as if I'd killed him with my own hands.

"I can screw if I'm bugging you," Duane added.

I felt horribly alone, but didn't necessarily want to *be* alone. "It's cool," I told him. "Stick around if you want."

"Sweet." He dug a small bottle out of his coat pocket, took a long swig, then offered me some. When I declined, he returned it to his pocket and slid up alongside me. "You all right, Stan?"

I looked into his glassy, bloodshot eyes. "Not sure."

With a muffled grunt, he sat down on the sand. "Bad night?"

"Been having lots of them lately."

"Maybe I can help."

"I appreciate it, but—"

"I see a lot of shit," he interrupted. "I know a lot of shit. Sometimes being invisible ain't so bad, you know? People see me, but they don't want to, so I disappear. I'm not really gone, though. I'm still there. Watching, noticing, hearing things other people miss, things they don't think I see or notice or hear. Even if I do, I don't matter, so who gives a shit anyway, right?"

I sat down, joining him on the sand.

"But I know a man with the Devil biting at his heels when I see one, tell you that much. I know it 'cause I been trying to outrun that bastard for years too. Opens your eyes though, don't it? Like I say, you get so you see things everybody else misses. Like the other night, that *was* you I saw."

"Yeah," I admitted. "It was."

"But it was somebody else walking around in your skin." He scratched at his crotch. "Things go on in this world of ours nobody sees. 'Cause it's not our world, Stan, not really. Like you said, *bad dreams*. I have them all the time too. Have for years, mostly 'cause I see those things other people don't."

"What kind of things?"

"People that aren't them. Like you the other night."

I wasn't sure how deep I wanted to get into this with Duane, but he'd never been so cryptic with me before. "Someone drugged me," I told him.

"They're drugging all of us. One way or another."

"You know who these people are, Duane?"

"There's things in the dark, right beside us, around us all the time—even right now, in the light—only we can't always see them. Sometimes we can, or we think we can, you know? We get like a—a glimpse, right? Then you got those that make them strong, that pray to the things in the dark, you see what I'm saying?"

I stayed quiet and let him talk.

"World's been burning a long time. Me, I don't really give a shit no more. As you can tell from my lifestyle choices, I'm not the most optimistic motherfucker on the planet." He chuckled softly, found his ottle and had another pull. "But I wasn't always like this, man. Not always."

"Me neither."

"You can't win," he said sadly. "You know that, right?"

"Does it matter?"

He took another drink, then returned the bottle to his pocket. "There's a guy you should talk to," he said, wiping his mouth with his hand. "He's crazier than a shithouse rat, but he knows what he's talking about. Used to be a professor, that's why they call him that, The Professor. Long fall, no wonder he's crazy, but that don't make him wrong."

I didn't say anything, but could tell from Duane's expression he sensed my apprehension.

"I know what you're thinking," he said, digging a crumpled pack of cigarettes from his coat. "Last thing you need is some homeless asshole telling you about some other homeless asshole who thinks he knows something."

"It's not that, I—"

"You always been good to me, Stan, kind. And not 'cause you want nothing."

I wanted to close my eyes as a way of shutting off, but I was afraid what I might find if I did. "I'm not a good person, Duane. I've done some terrible things."

"There's a war going on, and it's happening all around us. Most don't even know it, and it don't matter who believes or who don't, it just is. You got to talk to The Professor. He wrote a book once, got published and everything, but they ruined him, took him down. You need to know what he knows, Stan. I can take you to him."

"What's his name? His real name."

Duane thought for a moment, his eyes narrowing into a squint. "Sorry, I—you know I get confused sometimes, I—wait—it's Clinton. No, *Quinton*. Yeah, that's it, Quinton. Quinton Cassells. But don't nobody call him that."

"He's here in town?"

"Yeah, he's close. Real close."

"Who are you, Duane?" I asked. "Who are you really?"

"I'm just a friend, Stan. Been trying to watch out for you since we met."

"Am I dreaming? Is The Devil's Breath on me right now? Or have I just lost my fucking mind?"

Rather than answer, he gazed out at the ocean.

"This meeting with The Professor," I said. "Set it up."

Duane nodded, and together, he and I watched the sun rise, two lost souls trying to find our way through the madness and out of the dark.

Neither of us spoke again.

A while later, I left him and walked back up to the cottage. The neighborhood was quiet, and although there were no longer people watching from the shadows—at least none I was able to see—I could still feel their eyes on me.

I found Sophie already up and busy at the stove. She looked better, like she'd actually gotten some sleep, but was still a bundle of nervous energy and clearly relieved to see me. "Hey," she said to me from her position at the stove. "I woke up and looked for you and—I—when you weren't here, I—I was worried."

It had been years since I'd come home to anything but an empty house. No one had worried about me in a very long time. "I didn't want to wake you."

She smiled reflexively. "Where'd you go?"

"Needed to look into something."

"Been gone long?"

"Little while. You didn't have to make breakfast."

"Wanted to. There wasn't much here but you had a couple eggs." Sophie pointed to the toaster on the counter. "Over easy with toast okay?"

"Sure," I said, though the idea of eating just then was repellent. "Thanks."

"There's coffee on too," she said. "Balthazar's in the bedroom. He's still freaked out but I think he'll be fine."

I pulled a mug from the cupboard and poured myself some. She already had a mug of her own going so I moved over to the table, slid the gun from my belt and placed it on the counter. "You manage to get some sleep?"

"Amazingly, yes." Sophie looked over her shoulder, and in doing so, noticed the pistol. "You're carrying a gun?"

I pulled out a chair and sank down into it. "Had it with me just in case."

"Noticed there's a shotgun in the bedroom closet too." She must've sensed something in my expression because then she said, "I was hanging up a few of my things, I—I didn't mean to pry or—"

"It's cool, don't worry about it."

Sophie flipped the eggs, sprinkled both with black pepper, then slid them onto plates and joined me at the table.

I reached out and gently touched her wrist. "You okay?"

"I've felt safer in my life, but I'll be all right. What about you? You look even more troubled than you did last night."

"I'm sorry, Soph. For all of this."

"Eat," she said softly. "Before it gets cold."

We both sat there a moment looking at the plates, neither of us touching the food. Then our eyes met and we exchanged awkward smiles.

"It looks great," I finally said. "Smells even better, but I…"

"Aren't you hungry?"

Even as I grabbed my fork and forced down some egg white, flashes of Chic's horrified face drifted past my mind's eye. "It's really good."

"So where did you go? What happened?"

"The less you know, the better. Okay?"

She nibbled her toast. "Little late for that."

I had a sip of coffee and did my best to force the visions of Chic's convulsing body from my head. After a few more bites I pushed the plate away and sat back, my stomach already gurgling and revolting against the intrusion. Calmly as I could, I explained what had happened during the night. By the time I'd finished, Sophie had stopped eating too, her face pale and eyes wide.

"Are you sure he was dead?" she asked a moment later.

"Trust me on this."

"Jesus." She reached for her cigarettes and a lighter. "If anyone saw you going in or coming out of there—"

"No one did. Except for…" I explained about the dark figures hiding in the alley and at the top of the street. "I don't know who they were, never got a good look at them, but obviously they're linked to this and were either following me or Chic. There's no other way they could've known I was there."

Sophie stood up, unsure of what to do. "And this drug, this—what was it?"

"The Devil's Breath."

"Right, that. It sounds insane, like it couldn't possibly exist."

"I still don't know what any of this has to do with me. Chic said I was *chosen*."

"Okay, glad that's not too creepy at all." She lit her cigarette, then hugged herself. "And more happened, they did something else to you when you were under the influence of this drug?"

"Yes, I just can't remember much. Flashes, bits and pieces, it's like trying to remember a dream you can't quite get hold of."

Sophie moved to the counter. She'd brought her laptop with her. Grabbing it, she returned to the table and fired it up, taking one hard drag on her cigarette after another until the computer was ready for use. "Okay," she said, eyes gliding back and forth across the screen. "It is a real thing. The Boracherro tree, Colombia, the whole bit. It's like something out of a movie. And you're telling me they've got a super version?"

"Developed in labs by God knows who. Chic said it was tied to the powerful, and that he and the others he was involved with were all low-level people."

"So they're criminals but like a—what—a cult?"

"See what you can find on Saturn. Start with the god."

Sophie typed a moment, then clicked a link and a page popped up. A painting at the top of the page showed a depiction of the god Saturn.

On the wall, a crude painting of an old man lords over me.

"What's the matter?" she asked in response to my apparent reaction.

Even in limited light, I see he is sitting on a throne of sorts.

"I've seen this...him...before."

His hair is long and unruly, as is his beard. In his hand he holds a scythe.

"Where?"

"In those memories or dreams or whatever they are. There was a drawing or painting on a wall, but that's all I can remember."

"Says here that Saturn is the god of death, misfortune, isolation and fear. He's also the god of dark witchcraft and false prophecy. Time is his slave, and there's stuff about how he can control harvests or something." She flicked some ash on her plate. "Well, that's certainly cheery, he sounds like a charmer."

I moved my chair closer so I could better see the screen, ignoring the residue of screams echoing from the back of my mind. "Go on."

"The Phoenicians," she continued, "an ancient people who lived on the eastern coast of the Mediterranean until about 300 B.C., called him Molech, which means *king*, and worshipped him as a god. Says they sacrificed their children to him. By fire."

I grabbed our plates, carried them over to the sink, then dug around in one of the drawers until I'd found an old glass ashtray.

"Apparently the cross is the ancient symbol for the sun," Sophie explained. "The Phoenicians' symbol for Molech—or Saturn—was a black cross, which meant black sun. The symbol itself doesn't look like a regular cross though. It looks like the letter T, which apparently at that time was considered a cross."

"Yes," I muttered. "I remember the drawing of him was surrounded by symbols like that."

"Okay, well, to them, Saturn *was* the black cross. Or, the black sun."

My apprehension rising, I placed the ashtray on the table for her but remained standing. "So they're worshipping the same god these Phoenicians did?"

"Yeah, but hold on." Her fingers moved furiously across the keyboard. "According to a couple of these sites, there's an ancient Saturn cult in power today. Looks like it might just be a loony conspiracy theory, but who knows?"

"What's it say?"

"That the group is vast and comprised of elites, the rich, the famous and the powerful. Says they practice an ancient occult science based on a cult that existed before the Great Flood that figured out how to harness the power of the planets and use it to impede mankind. Says they accomplished this by using dark forces they conjured through blood sacrifices. God, this is some fucked-up shit." She crushed her cigarette in the ashtray and ran her hands through her hair, pulling it back and away from her face. "There's more. Something about how they use a *trinity of planetary mathematics*, whatever the hell that means, and ritual blood sacrifice to help them manipulate the world and control the population. There's a whole section here about Saturn once being our sun or something, and how the Earth and Saturn have something called a *coaxial relationship*. Let's see, what else. Something about how people's brainwaves synchronize with the electromagnetic waves coming from the Earth, and that changes in Earth's magnetic field are linked to changes in our brains. It's complicated, I—I mean—this is enough to make your head explode."

"It's hard to know what's real and what isn't," I said.

If Sophie heard me, she gave no indication. Instead, she continued staring at the screen as her finger slid across the mouse pad. "There's a part about black cubes and hexagons too, and how they relate to—"

"Black cubes?"

"That's what it says here anyway. How there are examples of black cubes everywhere, in all religions, in the media and in monuments all around the world. Says they're specific examples of the Saturnian cult marking their territories in a sense, showing the world they're in control and doing it right under our noses. It claims here that even graduation gowns and the square cap is an example, that its origins are based on this black cube thing. It has something to do with life, it—the cube is the building block in all of nature, according to this, and the Greeks believed the Earth was made up of cube-shaped particles. The cube shape, the triangle or pyramid shape and the All Seeing Eye, they're all important in this, I guess. Incarnation, the souls coming and going on the rings of Saturn, I—Christ—there's so much information here it's blowing my goddamn mind."

"Sophie," I said, "the club Chic mentioned was called The Cube."

"Holy shit."

"The business card that gets you in is all black, a black cube."

With a heavy sigh Sophie lit another cigarette. "I know I just put one out but my nerves are shot, so if you'd just let me sit here and get lung cancer without any commentary, I'd appreciate it." She returned her attention to the various websites, moving through them in an attempt to mine any additional information. "Listen to this," she said, adjusting her position. "In 1979, the *Voyager* spacecraft found a perfect hexagon over Saturn's north pole. In 2006, another craft called the *Cassini* showed that the hexagon was still there. Clouds move in a counterclockwise direction around its edge at sixty miles an hour. Since in these circles Saturn is known as the black sun, they call this hexagon The Black Cube, because a hexagon, when viewed three-dimensionally, is a cube. To those who believe in and worship Saturn, the discovery of the hexagon is further proof of their place and power in the universe and in the nature of Man and all things."

We were both reeling.

"What the fuck, Stan?" Sophie looked at me with equal parts confusion, fear and disbelief. "Can this be real?"

"It's hard to believe there could be this much information so easily available without either of us ever hearing about it, but—"

"That seems to be a recurring theme," she interrupted. "That it's all right out in the open but people don't see it or realize it, and even if and when they do, nobody believes it. Those who do are considered nutcases."

"Whether any of it's real or just a bunch of crazy theories is another story," I said, "but there's something to this."

"At a minimum, some seriously deranged people exist who believe this shit."

I walked over to the back window and looked out at the path leading through the dunes to the beach. The heat was already rising, rippling and blurring the world as it rose from the sand like a mirage.

"It's crazy, but—Stan—if this is true, even some of it, then these people are even more dangerous than we thought. If it's all bullshit, then they're also sick in their heads. We're talking deeply insane here. And just in case you were wondering, neither option exactly bodes well for us." Sophie looked so lost and afraid, so vulnerable despite her strength. I wanted to put my arms around her and tell her I didn't have a clue either, that I was just as frightened and confused as she was but that everything would be all right. Instead, I remained where I was and motioned to her laptop. "Is there anything else?"

"Tons. It'd take days to go through these sites and all this information."

"Can you find anything about a Professor Quinton Cassells?"

Sophie typed it in. "There's a guy with a big website here, looks like he's got something for every conspiracy buff. Aliens, crop circles, shadow governments—the whole megillah—and apparently they did an interview a few years ago with someone by that name. He wrote a book called *Saturn's Gate*, and according to this, it ruined the guy's career. Says he used to be a respected college professor but after trying to spread the truth about what he called 'The Saturnian Death Cult Conspiracy,' he fell off the radar. He's not the only one to put out this kind of book, but he's local, or was at the time he wrote the book. His bio says he lived in Cambridge. According to this site, Cassells dropped out of sight completely and no one's seen or heard from him in almost five years. They're not even sure he's still alive, but this site seems to think he's in hiding or something. He's probably a crank, Stan."

"He could be," I said. "Or he could be someone who can help."

"How did you hear about him?"

I didn't really want to tell her, but we were already on our way down the rabbit hole, what difference could it possibly make now? "I think Duane knows where to find him."

"Duane?"

"Yeah."

She closed the laptop and sighed. "As in, Duane the homeless guy you know?"

"Yes."

"He just happens to know this guy?"

"Apparently."

"And you don't find that a little strange? Fuck that, *a lot* strange?"

"Look," I told her, "right now everything feels like a nightmare I can't find my way out of. Nothing makes any goddamn sense anymore. Maybe it never did. But maybe—just maybe—this guy can help me sort out the fact from the fiction and show me a way out of this. Maybe Duane's known what was going on for a long time, I don't know. But until I hear from him, I need to check out that club, The Cube, and see what I can find."

"Think it'll be open on a Sunday?"

"Only one way to find out."

"Fine. I'm coming with you."

"No you're not."

"Stan, spare me the macho hero bullshit, okay? I can handle myself."

"It's not that. I'm just better alone. And I don't want you to get hurt."

"That's sweet, I don't want you to get hurt either."

"Soph—"

"Come on," she said, grabbing her purse and moving past me, a cigarette dangling from her mouth and smoke trailing from her nostrils. "I'll drive."

14

BLOOD. EVERYWHERE. ON THE *walls, the floor, the breaks in the ceiling where the spiders have not congregated...*

I want to stand. I want to run. But all I can manage is a crawl along the wet and sticky floor. It smells here. Like death, it—it smells like death. Things that are meant to be inside the body have come outside. They've been strewn about, draped across the window like bloody vines, and the mirror that once hung on the far wall now lies in the corner opposite me, smashed to pieces.

The Dark One watches from the wall, his likeness painted there in blood.

On another wall, the all-seeing eye within a pyramid, leering at me like the master it serves, it too finger-painted in blood and an array of bodily fluids.

The screams have stopped. It's quiet now. So quiet I can hear the spiders clicking and writhing above me. And beyond the blown-out window facing the ocean, a gentle rain has begun to fall, rolling in off the Atlantic in the distance as the fog and mist slowly dissipates.

I keep moving. I have to keep crawling across the disgusting floor, despite the wetness squishing beneath my palms and the way my legs slide with each attempt.

Eventually I struggle my way to a small basin-like piece of cracked porcelain in the corner I hadn't noticed before. Though concealed in shadow, it too is spattered with blood. Things float in its shallow tub, horrible things bobbing in a soupy black mixture of bile and gore.

A whisper...did someone just whisper in my ear? Did I feel breath just then, a sudden hot and fetid exhale against my throat as words I do not understand were muttered from the shadows?

I look around frantically, but there's no one there. I'm alone with my terror, the blood and filth, alone with a demented king surveying his toys from a throne of horror and deceit.

Far enough from the center of the room, I can see that the smears of blood on the floor are not random, as I'd originally thought.

They form an enormous pentagram.

* * *

Following the GPS on Sophie's phone, we located The Cube on a side street that otherwise consisted of a few run-down vacant houses, several boarded-up and long-closed storefronts and an empty, garbagestrewn lot overgrown with grass and weeds. From the street, The Cube looked like it had been closed for years along with everything else in the neighborhood. A squat building with a flat roof and no windows, it was badly aged and painted entirely in black, as was the front entrance, over which hung a small red sign advertising the name of the establishment.

No one came to this part of Sunset anymore, and certainly not to this street in particular, unless they were passing through, lost, or if The Cube was their intended destination. This time of day, and especially on a Sunday, the area was likely even more deserted than usual, the sounds from the busier touristy section of town barely discernable here.

Three cars sat parked in a small dirt lot next to the building, but they were all older models and it was impossible to tell how long any of them had been there.

"I'm pretty sure it's closed," Sophie said.

"Probably, but I'm going to take a closer look. Stay here."

"But—"

"I mean it," I said firmly, and then, seeing her disapproval, added, "I need you here, okay? Especially if I get inside."

"Fine. But if you're not out in fifteen minutes, I'm coming in after you."

"If I'm not out in ten, stay put and call the cops." I waited until she looked me in the eye. "Understand?"

"Yeah, I got it," she said softly. "Just be careful, all right?"

I got out and leaned against the car, watching the area and waiting to see if anyone came out of the proverbial woodwork. No one did. I could smell the ocean here, the only reminder I was still close to home. It offered little comfort.

Satisfied with my recon, I crossed the street and approached the entrance to The Cube. The door was black like the rest of the building, which made it difficult to make out initially, but then I saw a small silver handle and a card slot to the left of it that, ironically enough, resembled the kind one would find at an ATM.

I gave the handle a pull but the door was locked. With another quick look around, I took the black card from my wallet and pushed it into the slot. A brief buzzing noise was followed by the sound of a lock disengaging, and this time, when I gripped the handle, the door opened without resistance.

It was so dark inside I had to reach out and touch the wall to my right to get my bearings as my eyes adjusted to the sudden lack of light. Slowly, the modest foyer, with its scarred black wall and ceiling and worn red carpet, came into better focus. On the wall to my left, two silver-framed black-and-white photographs advertised some of the musicians presumably playing there. A small and narrow hallway emptied out into the club proper, where I could see a bar and several tables illuminated by candlelight. Along the back wall was a stage on which a drum kit and piano sat, neither occupied.

As I walked into the lounge area, I noticed all the tables were empty, but two stools at the ornate, backlit and largely glass bar, undoubtedly the centerpiece of the room, were occupied, one by a muscle-bound man with a shaved head and the other by an older man in a cheap and wrinkled suit. Soft jazz played through speakers hidden in the walls and ceiling, and an attractive female bartender stood behind the counter watching me with indifference. Dressed in a black skirt and vest sporting a sparkly red bow tie, she and the rest of the place had a retro feel, like I'd stepped back in time and entered a small jazz club from another era.

The bald man looked over at me as I approached, a strange look in his small, dark, rodent-like eyes. The older man remained huddled over his drink, and while he hadn't looked up or acknowledged me, I could tell he was aware of my presence.

Although I was certain I'd never been here before, there was something familiar about the place that bothered me. I'd been in bars that weren't exactly welcoming before, but this was a different vibe. I felt more than unwelcome, I felt fear, and had no idea why. Masking it best I could, I selected a stool, leaned on the counter and gave the bartender a nod.

"How'd you get in here?" she asked.

"Walked through the front door," I answered.

She smirked, creasing her heavy makeup. With a long mane of red hair in a shade one could only find in a bottle, and her cartoonish figure, she was anything but intimidating, though she gave it her best shot. "This is a private club," she snapped, flashing a quick glance at the bald guy. "You need a card to get in here."

I held up the card.

The bald man slid from his stool.

"Easy, Teddy," the older man said without looking up from his drink.

I turned to face him but stayed seated, my eyes locked dead on his. "You heard him," I said.

"What you drinking, son?" the older man asked.

Rather than answer, I continued the staring contest with his buddy.

"*Teddy*," he said, louder this time. "Easy, I said."

Teddy rolled his shoulders the way gym rats sometimes do to loosen up, then returned to his stool. When he got there, he threw me one more sneer just to be sure I knew he was there if I wanted to pursue that angle.

I gave him a thin smile in return, knowing it would achieve what I wanted.

Once he broke eye contact, I turned to the older guy. His silver hair was cut close to his scalp and his deep brown skin was heavily lined and creased. Up close he looked a good deal older than I'd originally thought, and had the appearance of the grizzled old jazz musician he likely was. But there was a serious nature to this man, a darkness not just about him but in him that was genuine to the bone, and his eyes told as much of the story as I needed to know, because if looks could've killed, Teddy would've been dead. But the old man never said another word to him. Didn't have to. By the time Teddy returned to his drink, he'd bowed his head in submission beneath the weight of his elder's steely gaze.

"Folks around here call me Slide," the old man told me, and then he said to the bartender, "Get us a couple shots of Jack, would you, Dolly?"

"I'm good," I said. "I'm not here to drink. Looking for Felix."

"Don't know anybody by that name."

"How about you, sunshine?" I asked the bartender. "You know anybody by that name?"

She glared at me.

"All right then, *Clyde*," I said, "guess it's all on you. Where do I find him?"

"It's Slide." He sipped his drink, unfazed. "And a man should be careful about how easy he drops names like that. Never know who might be listening and taking note. Especially in places where a man got no business being in the first place."

I could feel myself continuing to transform, returning to this strange *other*, an old, violent, arrogant alternate self I thought I'd killed off and buried long ago. "I'll do my best to give a shit about that," I said. "Meanwhile, where is he?"

"Son, go on home," Slide said, his bloodshot eyes imploring me. "Forget all this, let it go and get on with your life while it's still yours to live, you hear?"

Still struggling to hold this other me in check, I dropped down off the stool and stepped back so I could keep both men in my line of sight, fully expecting Teddy to come at me. To my surprise, it was Slide who gathered his keys and came down off his stool. I wanted to question him, to push this man on what he knew, but the darkness in him left me off balance, and the darkness rising in me was even worse.

"I don't know how you got that card or who this Felix is or what you think you're doing in here, but believe me when I tell you this, friend. There are places in this world you don't belong, and you're standing in one of them right now. Go home, like I told you. Don't come back."

"He meant now." Teddy spun around and faced me, but remained seated.

I'd never seen these people before, but they knew me. They recognized me the same way Chic had. I could feel it.

"And leave the card," Teddy added. "That's club property."

I held it up like a prize. "Why don't you come get it?"

Teddy chuckled. "You just stupid or some kinda mental retard?"

I flicked it at him. The card snapped off his shoulder and fluttered to the floor. He never moved. This time I chuckled. Then I moved away, walking quickly out to the foyer, through the door and back into the warm and sunny light of day, my mind reeling and my heart crashing my chest with the subtlety of a sledgehammer.

As I knew he would, Teddy followed me out the front door, and just like years before, what came next arrived as a series of options. If things turned physical, I already knew what I was going to do. Right from the get-go, I'd be a move or two ahead of him. Like riding a bike, I thought, you never forget this shit. No matter how hard you convince yourself you have.

Across the street, I saw Sophie sit up in the car the minute I was outside, and could only hope she'd stay put. I gave her a look indicating that would be best but couldn't tell if she'd seen or understood it.

"Hey!" Teddy growled from behind me.

I stopped, faced him.

"What was that?" he asked.

"I'm not here to talk to you, asshole."

He flexed and took a step closer. "Well, I'm here to talk to you, slick."

"Unless you want to tell me where I can find Felix, I got nothing else to say."

"Instead of talking, maybe you should try listening."

"Can you take me to Felix or not?"

"I don't know who that is," he said, pointing a stubby finger at me. "But I'll tell you what I do know, dick cheese. You're fucking around with the wrong people and you need to get the hell out of here and never come back."

"I got no interest in you," I said. "I need to talk to Felix."

"You think I give a shit what you need?"

"Where do I find him, jackoff?"

Something in his eyes changed. They flashed a peculiar kind of satisfaction I hadn't expected. "You don't find Felix, bitch. He finds you."

"Well, here I am."

"Get out of here before you get hurt, granddad."

I didn't say a word. Didn't have to with guys like Teddy. I just smiled. Big. Big enough for him to understand that I was laughing right in his face and didn't give a shit if he knew it.

Taking the bait, Teddy lunged for me. I hit him in the base of the throat with the heel of my palm. Hard. Between the force of the blow and his forward motion, it stopped him dead. He gasped, shocked by both the speed and effectiveness of the strike, and brought both hands to his throat. Spinning away, he doubled over and gagged. As he staggered about, he began to cough until a long drool of spit dangled from his bottom lip nearly to the curb.

I could've kicked his knee out from there and given him the beating of his life once he was on the pavement, but I waited on him instead, taking a quick glance back at Sophie, who thankfully had started the car but hadn't gotten out.

"You let Felix know I'm looking for him," I said. "Understand?"

"Fuck yourself," Teddy said, his face flushed bright crimson.

Over by the front door of The Cube, Slide had just emerged, a cigarette dangling from his mouth. He saw what was happening, shook his head, then turned and slowly walked away in the opposite direction.

I crossed the street, waving to Sophie as I stepped off the curb. She pulled out and I hopped into the car.

"Holy shit!" she said. "That was awesome! You're a fucking badass!"

"Just a lucky shot he wasn't expecting." I pointed to Slide. "Follow him."

"I thought that guy was gonna kill you, he's huge!"

"*Soph*," I said, pointing. "Follow him."

"Yeah," she said, snapping out of it. "Right, right, I'm on it."

She drove, creeping along behind him as Slide walked to the next block and then the next. He never looked at us, but he knew we were there.

"Stay right on his ass," I told her.

"Is that other guy all right?" she asked, checking the rearview.

"He'll be fine."

It was then that I noticed the light had changed. It wasn't nearly as bright as it had been. At first I thought it was just my eyes adjusting, but dark clouds had begun drifting in off the ocean, blocking out the sun and bringing with them the threat of a summer storm.

Slide left the street and walked down a small embankment toward the railroad tracks that ran through town. Sophie pulled over and I got out and followed him on foot. This time she came with me and I didn't have time to tell her not to as I didn't want to lose him.

Down by the tracks were several small older houses that had been there for decades, along with a few abandoned brick ruins set atop expanses of cracked pavement overgrown with weeds and littered with trash and debris. It was an area I had driven by from a distance perhaps once or twice but had never ventured into until now.

"Stay close," I told Sophie. "No telling where he might be leading us."

After about a hundred yards or so, the pavement became dirt, and the weeds and overgrown grass were nearly knee-high. Near end of the road, where it all turned to forest, there sat two small run-down shacks, and the ruins of three more, leftovers from an earlier era when those who worked for the wealthy in this little seaside resort town lived in poverty on the literal edge of town in makeshift shacks, shantytowns of crude quarters. Now, decades later, this was all that remained.

Slide kept moving, walking at a slow and steady pace. He did not look back, even when he reached his shack. He climbed the three rickety steps, unlocked the door, then disappeared inside. But he didn't close the door behind him; instead, he appeared behind a screen door seconds later, watching us without expression.

We stopped in the patch of weeds that constituted his front yard.

I looked behind us to make sure Teddy or anyone else hadn't followed. We were alone. It felt like a completely different town, maybe even another planet, alone and desolate out here, yet only moments from the hustle and bustle of commercialism and the gleeful cries of tourists.

Through the screen, Slide mumbled something I couldn't quite make out, but the cadence led me to believe it was a prayer of some kind, though I couldn't be sure. His voice was a low and whispery grumble leaking through the dirty screen, and then he fell silent and continued staring at us. When he finally spoke at a volume and in a manner that was discernable, he said, "Sometimes the Devil gets a bad rap, son."

"How's that?" I asked.

The lids of his bloodshot eyes grew heavy, giving him an almost reptilian look. "Devil don't come to you," he said. "You go to him."

We all stood there a while in silence.

"If you're coming in," Slide finally said, "then come ahead."

I felt Sophie's hand take mine and hold tight. Together, we walked up the steps. Slide never opened the screen door, he just moved away, deeper into the shack.

As we stepped inside the dark little shell of a building, we were confronted with a strange smell, something similar to incense but stronger. There were beer cans and empty liquor bottles everywhere, an old acoustic guitar lay on a couch cluttered with spent food wrappers and old magazines, and on one wall hung two electric guitars and a few framed replica gold records, the cheap glass and plastic frames smeared and in need of a good scrubbing. A hexagon had been crudely painted on another wall, with several other strange symbols encircling it. Beyond the small main room was a narrow hallway that presumably led to a small bedroom. There was no kitchen, and I couldn't even be sure there was indoor plumbing, much less a bathroom.

"You think I'm some kinda animal?" Slide asked.

"What do you mean?"

"Of course there's a bathroom," he said. "I'm a poor man, but still a man."

Fear wrapped around me like a blanket. How the hell had he known what I was thinking?

"Lots of things in this world you don't understand." Slide dropped down onto the couch, scooped up the guitar and let it rest across his knees. "But you'll come to it. Same as the Devil, you'll come. Sooner or later, they all do. The meek ain't gonna inherit shit, son."

"I didn't come to any of this," I said. "You people chose me. You robbed me, you—"

"Never a shortage of fools," Slide said, taking his guitar up and strumming it slowly. In the otherwise quiet shack, it had a haunting sound. "They make mistakes. Talk when they shouldn't, get greedy when there's no need, don't notice when they should, when things go missing. Like a black card, maybe, or a quick trip to the ATM, yeah? It don't mean nothing, son. It all gets washed away. Ask your little friend in Brockton."

"I can't," I said. "Not anymore."

Slide smiled with his bloodshot eyes and quietly strummed his guitar.

"What do you people want with me?" I asked.

"*You people*? Nigger, please."

"I'm not here for jokes, Slide."

"You got no idea why you're here, son. If you did, you be running."

"What do you want? Why me? Why did you pick me?"

"Not for me to say. You had your chance to walk. You didn't."

Sophie pulled at my arm. "Let's get out of here."

"Didn't I tell you to go on home?" Slide asked. "Didn't I give you that chance?"

I held firm. "I want to talk to Felix."

"Do you now."

"Make it happen."

He did a quick riff on his guitar. "It all falls as it's meant to."

"Sophie," I said, pulling my hand free of hers. "Go wait outside."

"Aw, you gonna beat on a tired old man?" Slide asked, smiling.

"Please, Stan," Sophie said. "Let's just go."

"No, it's time to—"

"Strange thing, time," he said. "You don't know nothing about it. You only think you do."

I tried to remember what Sophie had told me in her research about Saturn. Something about time, but I couldn't remember.

"Time belongs to him," Slide said. "Does as he tells it."

And then it came to me, suddenly. *Time is his slave.*

"Saturn," I said.

He sat back, let the guitar rest, but a slow boil of anger bubbled just beneath the cool exterior he was trying so hard to achieve. "You get on your knees when you say his name, boy."

"I don't get on my knees for anybody," I said. "Much less some dime-store god a bunch of fucking freaks like you think is the Devil."

"Keep talking. Keep whistling right past that boneyard. Keep telling yourself you ain't afraid of the dark. Maybe sooner or later you'll believe it."

"The only one who should be afraid here is you."

"Snake don't fear the rat, son. Spider don't fear the fly. They set the trap and wait, let the prey come to them. And it always comes." He motioned to the door behind us. "*Always.*"

I slid over to the screen door and stole a quick look outside.

Standing in front of the shack in a line was Teddy and two other men.

All three were good size, and one in particular—the man in the middle—was huge. All three were dressed in black. Teddy and a man who could've been his twin, also with a shaved head, stood on either side of the third, a gigantic black man with thick braids that hung to the middle of his back. His iceblue eyes were nearly as startling as his massive, sculpted physique. I locked on to those eyes. He was clearly in charge of the trio.

I took Sophie's hand. "Stay behind me, understand? And don't say a word."

As Slide laughed softly, I pushed open the screen door and descended the steps with Sophie in tow. I felt her pull at me and glanced back. She'd crouched down and grabbed an apple-sized rock from the ground.

Before I could stop her, she'd thrown it at them. It connected with the shortest of the three and bounced off his smooth pate just below the ear. With a grunt, he brought a hand to his head and looked back at her menacingly. "Bitch, seriously? The fuck?"

"She do that again," Braids said, his voice a smooth baritone laced with a slight trace of Jamaican accent, "cut her fucking throat."

Grinning like an imbecile, Teddy pulled an enormous knife from his belt and held it up for both of us to see.

"Be cool, Sophie," I said without breaking eye contact.

"Yeah, Sophie," Braids echoed. "Be cool."

"She's just scared, this has nothing to do with her," I said. "Who are you?"

"Don't matter who I am. The Man need to see you."

"The Man?"

Braids nodded.

"And who's the man?"

"That don't matter neither. All that matter is he need to see you."

"She's got nothing to do with this," I said, motioning to Sophie. "Leave her out of it."

"Ain't up to me. She with you, so she coming too."

I held my stance, finally looking to the other two men. They were all gym rats and obviously partial to steroids, lots of them, and who knew what kind of training they had. I could fight, but I didn't stand much of a chance, and we all knew it. Besides, I wanted to meet Felix, and that was likely whom they were referring to.

"It'll be all right," I said to Sophie. "Just stay calm, all right?"

Sophie clamped her hands on my arm and I could feel her heartbeat thudding against my shoulder, but she never said a word.

"You don't give me no trouble," Braids said, "everything be good.

You fuck with me, ain't never gonna be good again. You feel me?"

"Yeah." I cocked my head toward Sophie. "But if anything happens to her, I'll kill everybody within reach. You feel *me*?"

Braids smiled, revealing chalk-white teeth. "All fruits ripe," he said, clearly amused, and then realizing I had no idea what that meant, added, "It's all good."

The third man moved behind us as Teddy took up position in front of us. Braids stayed the closest, right alongside us, and we all moved back across the lot to the dirt road and the large black car awaiting us.

It had gotten even darker now. The storm was closer.

Wind blew, disappearing into the forest as the stifling heat eased somewhat, succumbing for just a little while to the cool ocean breezes that generally came before the thunder, lightning and downpour that was surely on its way.

Snake don't fear the rat.

As we closed on the car, the ghostly sounds of Slide's guitar played, riding that same wind, and making promises of its own.

Spider don't fear the fly.

Promises of other storms, darker storms we'd walked right into.

15

WE RODE IN TENSE silence. Sophie and I were both loaded into the backseat along with the third guy, while Teddy drove and Braids took the front passenger seat. No one said a word, no music on the radio. It was getting darker so I couldn't make out much detail inside the car, but it smelled recently disinfected with a heady cleaner.

Once we'd left the neighborhood, I started to take notice of where we were. When we hit the main drag, it was still congested but starting to clear out as the imminent storm approached. I noticed a couple police cruisers parked at the entrance to the dock. We drove by without incident, traveling until we'd literally reached the opposite end of town. Soon we were barreling along a desolate and curving coastal road, and I knew then they were taking us down to the sand. There was nothing else out this way but dunes and beach, but it was an area few tourists knew about, and even locals rarely patronized due to the rocky shore-line, isolated location and difficult-to-maneuver dunes.

I wasn't sure what to think at that point, but no matter how I approached it, this wasn't good. I'd grown up in a coastal city. You took people to the sands for various reasons, none of them good. When I glanced at Sophie, she glanced back, and I knew she was thinking the same thing. I gave her hand a gentle squeeze in the hopes of reassuring her everything would be all right, but the expression on her face left no doubt how terrified she was. I was still angry with myself for allowing this to touch her, but it was too late for regrets, it had happened and now I had to focus on what might be headed our way.

The road narrowed and became less maintained. The car slowed but it was still a bumpy ride. Storm clouds had gathered to the point that headlights punched two long holes in the growing darkness ahead, but revealed little other than the tall grass along the dunes in the distance.

Slowly, the car came to a stop.

Braids and Teddy got out first, then opened both rear doors. Sophie and I got out on the driver's side, their cohort on Braids's side. The doors closed behind us, the sound echoing across the dunes and down toward the ocean. It was quiet, but for the distant rumble of thunder, and the smell of the ocean was strong here. The air was cooler now, and far less oppressive due to a steady wind blowing in off the Atlantic. The tall grass along the dunes swayed spookily in the darkness, the sound of their stalks brushing against each other like whispers.

Teddy lit a cigarette, cupping the flame with his hands as Braids pointed to a narrow path just off the road. I took Sophie's hand, kept her close, and with the three men following us, we walked carefully through the darkness, into the tall grass and up to the top of the nearest dune.

Sophie and I again exchanged troubled glances.

It was getting night-level dark, and the going was difficult. Once we reached the top of the dune, I could see down onto the beach, and a large bonfire burning below that lit up the growing darkness. Several shadowy forms were standing around the fire, one of them dancing despite the fact that there was no music playing. The others all stood stationary, staring into the flames. I couldn't make out their faces, or any detail at all, really, but I made a quick count of four people including the dancer, who was smaller than the others, moved like a woman and likely was one. Seven people total, six men and one woman. My odds had sucked to begin with, and they'd just gotten worse.

After a less-than-gentle nudge in the small of my back from Braids, Sophie and I started down the sloped side of the dune, moving toward the sand and fire and ocean. Nothing seemed real. We may as well have been walking along the surface of some alien planet. The rest of Sunset seemed that impossibly far away.

They could kill us out here, I thought, and no one would hear, no one would see and no one would be anywhere around to stop them.

When we reached the sand, we were instructed to stay where we were. Teddy and the other guy making up the bald duo remained with us while Braids went ahead to the giant fire and spoke briefly with one of the shadows standing before it.

At closer range, I could see the dancer was, in fact, a woman. Perhaps thirty, she was petite, with short, wild blonde hair, numerous tattoos and strikingly pretty Nordic features. Her glazed eyes bore heavy black makeup, her thin mouth was painted with bright red lipstick, and she danced slowly, seductively, as if in a trance.

Braids vanished into the shadows around the far side of the bonfire. The dark form he'd been speaking to slowly drifted into the light and transformed into a short but sturdy-looking man in his thirties. His hair was black and shoulder-length, blowing about in the breeze. Dark eyes looked me over, slid to Sophie, then returned to me.

"You know who I am?" he asked.

I had my suspicions, but said, "No."

The man motioned to the fire. "You know who they are?"

"Should I?"

The man stared at me but said nothing more.

I indicated Sophie. "There's no reason for her to be here, she's not involved in any of this."

"Why you want to come around causing problems and asking questions at The Cube?" Very subtly, he moved closer to us. "Why you bothering my friends?"

"I didn't bother anybody," I said. "You picked me off the street."

"I did?"

"We really going to play these games right now? I don't remember much, thanks to the drug you used on me. Found a card in the pants I'd been wearing, traced it to The Cube. No idea how I got it or what was happening. Must've picked it up without even realizing it when I was with you fuckers, Chic and whoever."

"I don't know anybody named Chic. And I don't know what the fuck you're talking about. Sounds like you got some sort of drug and alcohol problem to me."

"Yeah, well, we've all got our crosses to bear, huh?"

"That cross is gonna get a lot heavier if you're not careful."

Sophie tightened her grip on my hand.

"Yeah, I keep hearing that, but like I said, whatever this is, you people brought me into it. I was on my way home from work, minding my own business. So I'll tell you what. How about we cut the shit and you tell me what I'm really doing out here?"

The man glanced at Teddy and the other goon behind us. I knew what was coming, and braced myself, but rather than hit me, Teddy punched Sophie in the kidneys. She made a squeal of a grunting sound as she dropped to her knees in the sand, her hand breaking free of mine.

I spun and slammed the point of my elbow as hard as I could into Teddy's face. The cigarette was still in his mouth when I hit him, and he staggered back in a spray of orange sparks. Before I could do anything else, the other guy was right next to me, a Glock pistol pressed tight against my cheek.

After several tense seconds, the man waved him off. He returned the gun to his belt and attended to Teddy, who was down on one knee, rocking and groaning in pain while trying to stop the blood gushing from his shattered nose.

I crouched down next to Sophie, who had slumped forward onto her face, and put a hand on her back. "You all right?"

She straightened up, and with tears in her eyes, nodded.

Standing, I turned to the leader, my anger boiling and my fists clenched but held down at my sides. "You Felix?"

More staring.

"I'll take that as a yes," I said. "I got no idea what any of this has to do with me. All I was trying to do was figure out where my money went and what happened during that night, okay? That's it. But if anybody puts one more hand on her, this whole area turns into a murder scene. Maybe you, maybe me, maybe both, maybe some of your clowns, but somebody's dying on this beach anybody so much as looks her way again, got it?" I gave him my best dead stare right back. "*Fucking* try me, pal."

A smile curled his mouth. "Feels good, doesn't it? Anger. Rage."

I reached down, helped Sophie back to her feet. Over by the fire, the blonde freak was still spinning around and gazing at the blackening sky.

A shadow passed across Felix's already dark face. It bore several scars and was covered in black stubble, but he'd once been a nice-looking man. He wasn't physically intimidating, but his was a powerful presence. This was a serious man and no one to be trifled with. But he also knew the same thing was true of me. He could see Hell in my eyes, and I in his. My time on the streets had been years before, but once someone had that stamp, it was there for life. Faded and rusty as it may have been, it remained, a badge of honor those who possessed it recognized in each other and, to at least some degree, respected. Felix was in control, there was no question about that, but I could make things messy if I decided to be a pain in the ass, and we were both well aware of it.

"It's all a bad dream," Felix said.

"Who the hell are you?" I asked.

"We're his saints. You'll pray to us one day."

"You think your horror movie Devil bullshit scares me?"

"Twig on a river, buddy, that's all you are." Suddenly his eyes were alive and lustful. "Control is an illusion, it's all playing out no matter what you do. Don't you know yet that you already belong to us?" Felix raised his hand, one he'd kept by his waist since we'd gotten there, and slowly released a handful of sand into the night. "We're everywhere. Standing right next to you even when you think you're alone." The sand rode the wind, blowing away into the gathering darkness. "Thing about our lord is, by the time you know he's there, you're already his, already in flames."

"What the hell would you want with someone like me?"

Felix didn't answer, and at that point, I didn't much care. I still wasn't sure we'd be getting out of there any time soon—if ever—and all I wanted was to get Sophie as far away from these people as possible. To my right, Teddy and the other ass stood glaring at me, Teddy still clutching his bloody nose. I glanced at them but kept my focus on Felix. They were his lapdogs and would only attack on command. Until then, I didn't have to worry about them.

"You think it's me you got to worry about?" Felix finally said, stone-faced. "Or any of them? Is that what you think?"

"Your buddy Chic told me—"

"From what I hear, he's done telling anybody anything."

Cackling with laughter, the blonde woman spun around the side of the bonfire, arms out at her sides and her head thrown back in ecstasy.

"You weren't always some dishwasher," Felix said so quietly the roar of the nearby ocean almost muffled it completely. "But that's what you are now. This is beyond you in ways you can't even imagine. Shit, in ways I can't even imagine. So fuck your girl, wash your dishes and stay out of places you don't belong. It's already over. The world is ours, always has been."

As if on cue, thunder boomed, and a giant blue spear of lightning crackled, tearing across the sky and splitting the horizon as it stabbed down into the ocean.

"Your time's up, and it belongs to us. It belongs to *him*. And there isn't a goddamn thing you can do about it. But I'll tell you this." Felix leaned a bit closer. "You see me again, you're gonna bleed, understand?"

I nodded.

He turned to his associates. "Take them back to where you found them."

16

UNTIL THEY DROPPED US off and drove away, I couldn't be sure they weren't going to kill us. But once we were back on the road near Slide's shack where we'd left the car, and they had gone, I knew we were all right, at least for the time being.

Without a word, Sophie and I got in the car and headed out of there. I drove this time. Slow and steady, my mind still wrapped in a dull haze like I'd just risen from a long, nightmare-filled sleep.

Moments later, we stood outside my cottage in a slow rain, stunned and disheveled. It was later in the day but with the storm and darkness growing it was hard to tell exactly what time of day it was. I looked down to my wrist but I wasn't wearing a watch. Where the hell was my watch?

Sophie seemed to be wondering the same thing as she inspected her wrist, running her fingers along the bone where her watch apparently should've sat.

"Is your back all right?" I asked.

"It hurts, but yeah, I'm okay."

Everything seemed foggy, slow.

"We should go inside," I said softly.

With a vaguely controlled look of panic, she followed me to the door. Once we were inside, despite the cooler air in the cottage, I felt a hot instinctive rush of uncertainty and fear. Something was wrong, something here, *inside* the house.

And then Sophie uttered my name in a small and shaky voice.

On the floor, in what appeared to be blood, they'd painted an enormous pentagram. We were standing in the center of it. Smeared on the kitchen walls were various symbols that looked like those from my dreams, and on the counter sat a strange talisman crudely fashioned from sticks and string to form a figure sitting on a throne.

"Balthazar!" Sophie frantically searched the cottage, disappearing into the bedroom.

How the hell had they gotten in here? The door was locked and there was no damage to the lock or door frame. I stood stunned and trying to understand what was happening, my eyes moving from the symbols to the stick figure on the counter to the pentagram at my feet.

Sophie emerged from the bedroom holding her cat. "He was under the bed," she said breathlessly. "H-He's okay."

I was relieved he was all right as well.

"Why would they do this?" she asked.

"Maybe that's all this was," I said, "a reason to get us out of here so they could do...whatever the hell this is."

She took everything in, nuzzling Balthazar's head and cooing to him softly. "It's obviously a warning."

"I think it's more than that," I said. "It's a ritual. They performed some sort of ritual and this is what's left of it."

"My God," Sophie sighed. "This is insane. I—I don't know if I'll ever be able to feel safe again."

"Soph, do you wear a watch?"

"Yeah," she said, considering her wrist again. "But I guess I forgot it at home."

"Are you sure?"

"No."

I held my arm up. "I don't have mine on either."

"I don't know what to do." Sophie looked so small and helpless just then, her strength and humor, so evident before, shadows now. "I want to sleep, I—I just want to lay down and close my eyes, but I'm afraid."

"I'm going to clean this up," I muttered.

"I'll help."

But we didn't. We just stood there.

Rain sluiced along the windows, blurring the world outside even more. Thunder groaned in the distance, and a sudden gust of wind shook the cottage. Nothing seemed real, and like Sophie, all I wanted to do was sleep, as if somehow putting my head down and closing my eyes would make everything all right again.

I took her by the hand, and together we walked into the bedroom. It was darker in there, the lights off and the blinds closed. She placed Balthazar on the bed and slowly undressed until she was down to her panties and bra, then she slipped under the covers and lay there snuggled up with the cat and watching me with sad, tired eyes.

Every thought and movement felt as if it were occurring by rote. Though I really didn't want to just then, without even knowing why, I undressed and crawled into bed with her.

Sophie's body was warm and soft, and her hair felt nice against my chest as she snuggled closer and let out a quiet little mewling sound. The cat moved up onto the pillow above our heads and lay down, purring furiously.

I'd never felt so utterly exhausted in my life.

There was a sudden chill in the room. Curtains I didn't at first recognize fluttered as a cold breeze blew through the partially open window on the far wall. I snuggled closer, rolling onto my side as she turned her back to me so we could spoon.

"It's freezing," she said.

"It's not so bad," I said, nuzzling the back of her neck with my lips.

She moaned softly, a gentle little sound of inconvenience and subtle discomfort, and then ground her backside against me, closer still.

One hand found her waist, the other I draped across her. "See?"

"It woke me up," she said.

"I didn't know you were already asleep."

"What else would I be doing?"

"The cold woke you?"

"That and you were talking in your sleep."

"But I'm awake, we—we just got into bed."

She rolled back, faced me. "Who's Sophie?"

I looked into the beautiful blue eyes of my ex-wife, Linda, and felt myself spiraling away, tumbling down into a void of darkness so deep and profound I couldn't be sure I'd ever find my way out of it. Maybe I wasn't meant to. I began to shake, but not from the cold.

"Linda." I put a hand on either side of her head, gently brushed her hair from her face. I could feel myself shattering, breaking apart, and yet I held on tight, wanting it to be her, wanting it to be me.

She touched my face with familiar hands, traced my cheeks with her fingers and studied me as if she'd never seen me with such clarity before. "What do you do at night, Stan?" she asked. "Where do you go?"

I wanted to answer but couldn't.

"Who's Sophie?" she asked again.

"No one, I—I must've been dreaming."

She gave a little pout, but this was more serious than that. "I can always tell when you're lying to me. I always could. You know that, don't you?"

"Yes."

"Then tell me the truth."

I swallowed so hard it was audible. "I don't know anyone named Sophie."

She continued to hold my head in her hands, and through a slow exhale of breath whispered, "I love you."

"I love you too."

I turned away and rolled from bed. My bare feet hit cold floor. Not the cottage floor. *I'm dreaming*, I thought. Or was I dreaming until now? This was our house, our home, where Linda and I live with…

"Where are you going?" Linda asked. "Stay, snuggle, it's cold."

"I'll be right back." I stood up.

"Stan, we need to talk."

I looked back at her and nodded, then shuffled out the door and into the hallway. The house was dark and quiet, but the moment I took a step toward the bathroom at the end of the hall, a small figure emerged from the bedroom across from ours.

"Daddy?"

That voice. That sweet little voice cut me right to the bone, all the way down in a single slash. My entire body trembling, I watched Olivia pad from the shadows in her little pajamas, hair mussed and hanging down and her eyes still heavy with sleep. She was alive and healthy and the most amazing and beautiful thing I had ever seen. Tears filled my eyes. I cleared my throat and struggled to find the strength to speak to her.

"*Daddy?*" she said again.

I scooped her up, held her tight and began to weep. She felt and smelled and sounded just like I remembered her. She was real again. "Baby, baby, baby," I said, peppering her face and head with kisses. "My precious baby, I—I missed you, I—I missed you so much, I—Daddy loves you, baby, Daddy loves you."

"Why are you crying, Daddy?"

"I'm just happy, I—I'm happy to see you is all."

"How come you're up?" she asked, giggling, then rearing back a bit in my arms so she could get a better look at me.

"What are *you* doing up?" I asked. "You should be asleep, little lady, it's late."

"Don't be sad, Daddy." Her tiny fingers wiped the tears from my eyes, then stroked my cheeks, her big eyes studying me much the way her mother had just moments before.

"How could I be sad if I'm with you?"

"What happened to your face?"

"Nothing, I…"

At the end of the hallway, I saw him. A man. Not just any man, not just one man, all of them. This single being somehow represented them all, and I knew this, I felt it as deeply as I had ever felt anything. His face was largely masked in shadow, but his mouth opened and dark blood slowly ran out of his mouth and down over his bottom lip, coursing across the front of him in a gurgling frothy mess.

I held Olivia tight and backed away toward the bedroom, unable to tear my eyes from the bloody vision at the end of the hallway, which was morphing and suddenly writhing about violently as if throttled by phantom hands. The blood sprayed the wall as I pushed my daughter's face down to my shoulder so she wouldn't see, and I remembered. I remembered who all these men were because I could hear their voices, their pleas, their cries, their horror and agony.

It left only my shame, my guilt. All of it there in puddles and swathes of blood as black as coal.

And then my baby was limp in my arms. *Sleeping, she's only sleeping,* I told myself as I backed into the bedroom and swung the door shut, kicking it closed with my foot. *She's asleep and everything's going to be all right because this is my life, what it's supposed to be. And this is who I'm supposed to be. This is happiness, ours and ours alone.*

And it was dying right before my eyes, being obliterated for my sins. Again.

Please! Christ, please! Stop, I—I'll do whatever you say, just stop!

I closed my eyes, saw my fists smashing, my boots kicking and stomping, my weapons cutting and cracking and maiming. On that lonely stretch of sand, in those filthy alleys, empty pool halls and desolate backrooms, their blood flowed and their pleas went unanswered. Now, so did mine.

Mercy was a myth, a bad joke told in a room full of thieves and degenerates.

She was so small, so impossibly tiny and delicate, my beautiful little girl, limp in my arms like some boneless stuffed *thing*, dead as the day we buried her in that obscene little white coffin.

Linda was sitting up in bed, her knees drawn in close and her chin resting atop them as she cried softly. "Put her down," she said, sobbing. "Leave her alone, just—for God's sake—*leave her alone!*"

But I couldn't. I held her even tighter, closer, so I wouldn't see her face.

A strange clicking sound overhead drew my attention. I slowly looked up.

The spiders, a blanket of them covering the ceiling…

"Don't move," I whispered.

"You think they can't hear us?" Linda laughed humorlessly, her tears leaving long black streaks of eye makeup along her cheeks. "You think they don't know *exactly* what's happening?"

"Please…I…"

"What happened to your face, Stan? What happened to your *goddamn* face?"

The bedroom door shook. Someone—something—on the other side pounded on it violently, rattling it in its frame until the wood began to crack and splinter.

The door held, but from beneath it came blood, gushing and running into the bedroom and pooling at my feet in great crimson puddles.

Linda began to scream at me. Crawling to the edge of the bed like a rabid dog, teeth bared, she screamed with such rage I could not understand a word she was saying.

And then came the rain…a rain of angry black spiders.

* * *

I never killed anyone.

But you were there. You did nothing to stop it, so you might as well have. I…

Johnny Fitz, strutting about and waving the gun around like some psychotic in a bad movie. Bathed in sweat, he rages on and on as the poor bastard we brought here cowers in the corner. Fenway Dave and I stand off to the side, watching the blown-out doorway and alley beyond, the abandoned factory like something out of the horror story our lives have become.

"You know, right?" Fenway Dave whispers to me, his hands shaking from too much coke and the rush of understanding this time will be different than the others.

I shake my head no, but I do understand. I'm lying and fooling no one.

"It's not my call," Fitz tells the guy.

"Please," he says, the word slurred due to his split lip and missing teeth sustained during the beating we've given him. "I don't—what do you want me to do? I'll do it, I'll do it, please—"

"You believe this fucking guy?" Fitz laughs like the madman he is, coked out of his mind and ready to do what he's been told to do, what he will never be able to reverse or escape should he actually go through with it. "Like I got a choice!"

Like Fenway Dave says later, Johnny Fitz was right, there never was a choice. Word came down. You go, you get it done, you move on. We went there, we took him there and we knew damn well what would happen, what would be done to him. Unlike all the others before him, he wasn't supposed to go home. We couldn't get high enough or drunk enough to change that, because this time it's not about an unpaid vig, it's about stealing from those no sane person steals from, a corner-level drug dealer skimming and dying for a few dollars. It's about a small-time crew of thugs like us with a chance to make a mark and move to another level.

I just want to be gone from here. Gone from them, all of this. I want this horrible evil to leave me alone, unaware that I will never cleanse myself of such filth.

It isn't possible.

"Please," the poor soul says again, this blob of beaten and swollen flesh still hoping he can talk his way out of what has become his fate. "Please, man, I..."

I walk across the room to Johnny Fitz, my arms out.

"Stan," Fenway Dave says from behind me. "Don't."

But I've convinced myself I'm about to say something so poetic, so profound, that it will stop this madness and allow all of us to walk away. I can fix this.

I open my mouth to speak, and Johnny Fitz looks me right in the eye, smiles his shark smile and shoots the guy in the head.

The blast is deafening, and my ears are still ringing even as the side of the man's skull explodes, spraying the wall and my face and neck with blood and bodily fluids. The man slumps and collapses forward onto what's left of his face, dead before I fully process what has just happened.

"Okay?" Johnny Fitz says, screaming it at me for some reason. "Okay?"

The man's brains are on my face, in my mouth and eyes.

I'm as dead as he is. We all are.

Forgive me. Forgive us.

* * *

Through the horror, a pair of regal eyes blinked slowly, watching me with a detached air of superiority, perhaps even judgment. They were not human.

Balthazar.

I came awake—if what I'd been lost in was sleep—on the floor of the bedroom, curled up in the fetal position. Above me, on the edge of the bed, the cat watched with silent indifference.

Struggling to my feet, I steadied myself against the bed until my legs were under me and my head had cleared somewhat. I wiped furiously at my face and neck, but the blood was gone. Still hazy, I squinted at the bed to be sure who was lying in it. Sophie. Asleep. I reached out to gently stroke Balthazar's head but he reared back, growling as he arched his back and spit at me.

I backed away, staggered over to the window and leaned against the wall, this time steadying myself against the window frame as I opened the blinds and looked out at the storm.

At the head of the path that led to the beach below, Duane stood in the rain, watching the cottage.

17

THE WORLD HAD TURNED gray and chilly. Through the rain and mounting fog covering the coastline, Duane led me down across the dunes and onto the sand. We followed the waterline, the ocean rough and spraying us as white-capped waves crashed the beach. We eventually reached a long stone jetty and climbed over it, the rocks slippery and slick with rain. On the other side, another long stretch of beach awaited us. Duane looked at me briefly, then turned and continued on. I followed. Neither of us spoke.

When the beach finally ended, it gave way to a small dune and expanse of tall grass. Duane squatted down in the grass and began rummaging around as if looking for something. A moment later he stood up, bringing a sizable round piece of earth with him. A large hole had been dug into the earth, the cover a makeshift disguise of dirt and weeds fixed to a block of stone.

"Down there?" I asked above the howling wind.

Duane nodded sullenly.

"You fucking crazy?"

"It's the only way, Stan."

"Why?"

"That's where The Professor is. And he don't come out. Hole leads to tunnels, and the tunnels lead to The Professor."

"Man-made tunnels?"

"Yeah," he said, pulling the beginnings of a rope ladder from the hole. "I mean, I guess. I don't know how they got here or when. They just are."

"You sure the whole thing won't collapse in on us?"

"No." Duane motioned to the dark hole. "Use the ladder."

I approached the hole but couldn't see anything beyond it but darkness.

"Once you hit the bottom," Duane explained, "just move out of the way. I'll be right behind you. Don't worry, I got a flashlight so we'll be able to see."

Even though I knew I'd tucked the gun into the back of my pants before I left the cottage, I touched it anyway, letting my fingers rest against the weapon before I dropped down into the hole. Clutching the ladder, I slowly descended into darkness, a musty, earthy smell wafting all around me.

Once I'd hit the bottom, above me I saw Duane struggle into the hole, bringing the cover with him. He eventually got it in position, and as he slid it into place, we were submerged into total darkness. I could still hear the nearby ocean, echoing along the dirt walls the way it did when you listened to a seashell.

I heard Duane getting closer, then felt him brush against me as he reached the bottom. With a sigh, he slapped his flashlight a few times and it came to life, firing a hole of light into the other dark cavern. We had to crouch to continue, as the tunnel was not very high, and once we started, I realized it wasn't terribly wide either. I'd never been particularly claustrophobic, but the tunnel was so small and cramped I was on the verge of panic almost immediately.

"How far?" I grunted, watching the beam of light bouncing ahead of us.

Rather than answer, Duane quickened his pace, forcing me to do the same.

The tunnel wound to the left, then was straight for a while. The air was thin here, and the chill outside was long gone. It was getting harder to breathe the deeper we went, and then suddenly I felt a steady stream of air filtering down the tunnel in our direction.

The tunnel finally opened into a much larger area that had been dug out far more extensively and led to what looked like another series of enormous tunnels, these cement rather than dirt. It wasn't until we got closer that I realized they were some sort of old pipes that had been buried, probably giant drainage pipes that had once been part of a larger system but had either never been used or hadn't been used for their original purpose in eons.

Duane moved the light over to one of the three possible options, revealing something spray-painted across the wall.

YOU WORSHIP WHAT YOU DO NOT KNOW John 4:22.

"Through here," Duane said.

We stepped up, into the pipe, and followed it another fifty feet or so, until we reached another open area, this one littered with blankets, spent food tins and various items that indicated other human beings resided nearby, and had been here recently. We were able to stand upright now, and as Duane extinguished the flashlight, I saw a vast array of candles lighting the area instead.

On a pile of old blankets, partially concealed in shadow, a man sat watching us. He looked to be in his sixties. Skin pasty and pale, his gray hair was dirty and thin. Long fingers stroked an unkempt salt-and-pepper goatee.

I looked to Duane, but he was already heading back down the tunnel.

"Mr. Falk?"

"Yes," I said, turning back to him. "Professor?"

"Despite my doctorate," he said in a bored and somewhat bitter tone, "I haven't been a professor in a long time now. But I suppose I am *The* Professor."

Clad in dirty clothes and tattered sneakers, he didn't look much like a professor of any kind.

"The pay's atrocious," he continued, "and the benefits nonexistent. But it affords me these palatial quarters in this enchanting neighborhood." With a sigh, he rose to his feet. Tall and thin, his physique was long-limbed and gangly. He looked me over, scrutinizing me without subtlety. "Quinton Cassells."

"Stan Falk," I said, offering my hand.

"You look rather desperate." He gave my hand a quick shake. "Fear has a way of doing that to people." His hazel eyes were strained and distant, like a combat veteran who had seen horrors few could comprehend. "Despite the fact that I have dropped out of sight and live *off the grid,* as they say these days, people still seek me out. Privacy is a thing of the past, why should it be any different for me? Most of those I agree to see turn out to be completely out of their minds. Are you completely out of your mind, Mr. Falk?"

I knew we weren't alone, as I could hear breathing and could see shadows moving nearby but beyond the reach of candlelight. "I don't know," I answered.

"Those types tend to muddy the waters, as it were, and there unfortunately never seems to be a shortage of them. But there are those few who truly *have* seen behind the curtain. Doesn't mean they're not also crazy, but then, aren't we all to one degree or another? Madness. Insanity. They're about as real as it gets. That said, for obvious reasons, I need to be leery of anyone that takes the time and makes the effort to come to me."

"I'm not the enemy," I told him. "And I'm no threat to you."

"No, I don't imagine you are," Cassells said through a lengthy sigh, angling his head toward the blankets behind him. "Let's sit and talk a while."

I followed him over to the blankets and sat down. Papers and notebooks were scattered about, and an entire wall, from floor to ceiling, was covered with newspaper articles, printed pages, photographs and other information regarding Saturn, Saturnian cults and the like. The entire area smelled like body odor barely masked by some sort of generic air-freshener.

The Professor saw me looking at the wall. "Mine is an ongoing endeavor," he said, sitting across from me. "From what Duane told me, I'm confident you've already done some basic research on your own and know quite a bit, yes? After all, it's not as if I'm some master guardian of this information, it's all readily available and out there for anyone who chooses to look for it."

"Well, I—"

"*Dragons*," he interrupted, leaning forward.

"Excuse me?"

"How does one slay a dragon if dragons don't exist? How does one battle the smoky breath it lays down to conceal itself in if the beast is only myth, fairy tale, a bedtime story for children and the feebleminded?" He offered a slight smile. "The answer, of course, is in the question. Dragons *do* exist, but only in glimpses, flashes of nightmares and maddeningly indistinct memories at the very edges of human perception. You see, dragons *prefer* to be make-believe, to never reveal themselves completely, because doing so would leave no question, no deception or uncertainty, no paranoia. There would be only horror, stripped down and unburdened by the cover of darkness. But one must remember, that which is out in the open is also more vulnerable, which is precisely why dragons prefer the impunity of shadows."

He may not have been a professor in some time, but Cassells clearly hadn't lost his ability to lecture. College hadn't been in the cards for me, but I could picture this man in a vast hall speaking to large groups of students on a variety of subjects, and making even mundane topics interesting and entertaining.

I could also imagine him locked away in a padded cell.

"For me, dragons were nothing more than fantasy," he continued. "For years I fancied myself a skeptic. I worked to convince everyone how brilliant and discerning I was for not believing in much of anything, unaware that I was doing exactly what the dragons wanted. When I took the time to actually look into things, to do so without prejudice or preconceived notions but really and truly *investigate* what was out there, I came to understand rather quickly that what we see in this world is only the tip of the iceberg. Not only was there more beneath the surface, the majority of the iceberg was hidden there. And it was that part, that which we *couldn't* see, that did the damage and was the most dangerous. Why? *Because* it was unseen, and therefore dismissed by many as unimportant or even nonexistent. I wrote about this in my book."

Somewhere deeper in the tunnels, the sounds of a man and woman in the throes of a heated argument and screaming obscenities at each other drifted closer. Their voices carried, became louder and then more distant before finally fading to silence.

"Charming couple." The Professor sighed again. "And true thesauruses of profanity. You meet all kinds down here. Deeper you go, worse it gets."

"I haven't read your book," I confessed, "but I—"

"Few have. My life began to unravel the moment it was released. I lost my agent, and my publisher took the book out of print and removed me from their author roster without explanation. But that wasn't enough for those in the shadows. They were far from finished. They ruined me professionally and personally, they destroyed my life, Mr. Falk. They destroyed *me*. And all because I dared to tell the truth." He ran a hand through his thinning hair, his face twisted into a scowl. "I was accused of terrible things, I—I not only lost my career, but my family. I have an ex-wife and three children I haven't seen since those horrible charges, I…"

I didn't know what he was talking about but he apparently thought I did, so I let the silence that followed take hold and remained quiet until he continued.

"I would never hurt a child," he said, his eyes desperate and brimming with pain. "I would never be in possession of those terrible photographs and films they—they put them on my computer, Mr. Falk, I'm innocent. No one believed me, not my friends or colleagues, not even my family or my wife. No one. No one believed me."

"I do," I told him. I didn't have much choice at that point. "I believe you."

He stared at me a moment, licked his lips slightly, then sat back a bit. "Thank you," he said quietly. "You'd think people would've figured it out by now. They do the same thing over and over. Fight the power, Mr. Falk, disrupt the government or cross the powers that be, those who truly run this world, and rest assured, before you know it you *will* be accused of the most heinous crimes imaginable. Always to do with children, you see, because everyone can agree how awful that is, and few have any pity or patience when it comes to such things. People are so angry and upset they never stop to consider that perhaps the person in question is being set up, taken down using a surefire method. Even those who consider it can't take the risk, can they? These are crimes against *children* we're talking about, crimes that are unforgivable. It's a perfect weapon, and it works every time. They didn't have to do anything so dramatic as kill me. All they had to do was plant the right seeds and make the right accusations. Everyone else did the rest for them. Of course I denied all charges but I stepped down because otherwise it would've only gotten worse. Disgraced and looked upon as a depraved degenerate that enjoys sex with little boys was bad enough. I could've done prison time, and likely would have. But once I was ruined, had lost everything and was no longer a nuisance—which is all I ever truly amounted to in their eyes—they apparently decided that level of punishment was sufficient. Charges were dropped but the damage was done. It was over. I'd lost and they'd won. Again. I was relegated to guest slots on late-night podcasts and renegade radio programs patronized predominantly by the mentally ill, moronic conspiracy and religious theorists with childish beliefs and incorrect information, and those with IQs slightly lower than the average walnut. You see, the truth you seek is not only frightening, Mr. Falk, it's extremely dangerous. It's a loaded gun pressed to your temple with a trembling hand."

"I need to understand exactly what I'm dealing with, and why," I explained. "Professor, I need to know what you know."

He winced the same as if I'd injured him. Perhaps in some way I had. "What most today don't realize is that a relationship between mankind and Saturn—both the god and planet—has existed since ancient times. Many peoples worshipped Saturn. The Sumerians, Babylonians, Assyrians, Egyptians, Greeks and many others all worshipped him to one degree or another. Saturn led his brothers and sisters, the Titans, in a revolt against their father, and became king of the gods. Ring any bells? In biblical texts, there was a war in Heaven led by Michael, the Archangel, against the fallen one, Lucifer, who was leading a revolt against God, because he wanted to rule Heaven and earth. *'Now war arose in Heaven, Michael and his angels fighting against the dragon. And the dragon and his angels fought back.' Revelation 12:7.*"

"I've never been a religious man," I told him.

"The universe doesn't care. We worship him without even realizing it. *'All the inhabitants of the earth will worship the beast.' Revelation 13:8.*"

"Professor, with all due respect, I'm not here to listen to you quote biblical scripture."

"It's only one aspect," he said, waving a hand in the air between us. "Open your mind, Mr. Falk. *'My people are destroyed from lack of knowledge.' Hosea 4:6.* We cannot throw the baby out with the bathwater, that's what people don't understand. Those who believe ancient texts like the Bible or any other should be dismissed entirely are as ignorant and foolish as those who believe in them literally. I'm not even a Christian, but I see the value of Christian texts just as I can see the value of any other ancient text. There are truths in all of them, and no amount of falsehood that may exist alongside those truths can cancel that out. We are born of magic and deception, Mr. Falk, our origins, our history, this country—this *world*—all of it is wrapped in magic and what those who don't understand call myth. Myth is our reality and reality our myth. It makes no difference." He sprang to his feet and moved to the wall, pointing to various photos and papers there, the candles disturbed by his sudden movement, the flames licking the walls, the floor, us. "The point is, mankind has been worshipping Saturn—Satan—Lucifer—the Dark—whatever you want to call it, whatever label you want to give it—without even realizing it, for centuries. Evil. They worship evil. People believe they're worshipping God but it's not the god they think it is. Other people think they believe in nothing, in no greater power or any afterlife or spiritual realm, but by doing so they worship the same as the most devout, granting it power, again, without even realizing it. Why? Because we are deceived, Mr. Falk, that's why. Life, *this* life, is a deception, nothing more. It's a trick, a fake, a forgery, just like us."

I sat there, unsure of what to do or say. Cassells had gone from relaxed to the point of appearing bored to nearly coming apart at the seams in a matter of seconds.

"Prior to what most believe to be the Great Flood, nearly everyone practiced Saturn worship and considered him to be the supreme deity. He was represented by a symbol, the black cube." Cassells searched the wall frantically, then stabbed a finger at a grainy black-and-white photograph. "The very same symbol that was discovered on the north pole of the planet Saturn by NASA."

"And a hexagon seen three-dimensionally," I said, "becomes a cube, right?"

"Exactly!" Cassells pointed at me. "The hexagon is a common shape found in nature. Honeycombs and snowflakes are but two examples. If one looks at a hexagon three-dimensionally, however, it does in fact become a cube. And if that's not enough for most—and it isn't, because these are inconvenient truths—on the south pole of Saturn they have found another formation, something never before seen on any other planet, a constant hurricane-like storm, spinning and ringed with enormous clouds that create the shape of a human eye. It is a phenomenon unique to Saturn, a pattern and symbol found nowhere else. So we have a spinning hexagon over the planet's north pole and a spinning all-seeing eye over the south. As it is above, so it is below."

I wanted to find some truth in all this, but it was becoming increasingly difficult. Yet I knew—I *knew*—he wasn't lying to me.

"There are examples of black cube monuments and artworks all over the world. Denmark, Manhattan, Mecca, it's endless. And we all believe they represent something else. The entire planet has worshipped Saturn for thousands of years, and they don't even know it." He moved away from the wall, seemed to calm somewhat, then lowered himself back down onto the blankets.

In the darkness behind him I heard movement but couldn't make anything out. What sounded like a man muttering came and went so quickly I couldn't be sure if I'd heard or only imagined it.

"We've all been deceived, Mr. Falk. We worship the beast, all of us. Even those who think they worship nothing at all. The media, the world of entertainment, the power elite, they keep us focused on other things, distractions and explanations we all know deep down aren't right, aren't true. Yet we accept them, and in some cases fight for them, kill for them, become sheep for them. They don't want us to know what's really going on. Not yet. And that's fine with most, because they don't want to know. They're so swept up in their arrogance they wouldn't believe it even if it were right under their noses, which in many cases, it is."

I sat forward, rubbed my eyes and noticed an open can of soup near my feet, a white plastic spoon lying next to it.

"And yet, somewhere deep down," he continued, "if we're honest, we can feel it. Something's not right with the world, with us. We can sense it, and that feeling is growing stronger in each and every one of us. But we ignore it. We make excuses because only the crazy and foolish dare wander down that dark little rabbit hole, Mr. Falk. The rest whistle past the graveyard, convinced there's no such thing as ghosts, even as the hair stands up on the backs of their necks. The Brotherhood of Saturn still exists today. It never stopped existing, never weakened. Since ancient times it's only grown stronger, more powerful. It has a long history, and it's always been with us, just like the lord it worships, both are passed down from generation to generation. They're still in power, the elite, working behind the scenes, in those shadows where the dragon prefers to be. '*For our struggle is not against flesh and blood, but against the rulers, against the authorities, against the powers of this dark world and against the spiritual forces of evil in the heavenly realms.' Ephesians 6:12.*"

"So what's the point?" I asked. "What are they hoping to accomplish? Domination, control, what?"

"They've already accomplished those things. What they're trying to do now is to open the door, a portal, to usher in their god. Saturn. The cube is a doorway through which he will come. The blood sacrifices are what make it possible. Those they conduct quietly through their rituals, and those on a much larger scale we've seen over the last few decades. Wars, disasters, supposed attacks, it's all part of a larger picture, a greater plan." The Professor leaned his head back and looked at the darkness above us. "They're trying to weaken the Earth's magnetic field to help open the gate. They need to manipulate and control us, but they need to do the same with space, time and matter. You see, people's brainwaves can synchronize with the rhythm of electromagnetic waves generated in the earth's ionosphere."

"I don't—you're losing me, I don't know what any of that means."

He closed his eyes. "Changes in Earth's magnetic field are directly connected to changes in the brainwaves and nervous systems in human beings. The theory, their belief, is that if that energy could be channeled, it would allow for control over the human race *from within*. Horror, bloodshed and chaos have been shown to weaken not only human resolve, but Earth's magnetic field as well. So through the horror, the blood and death, the constant barrage of negativity and darkness, comes a weaker magnetic field, and in theory, a weaker population easier to control and deceive." He sat forward and held my gaze. "*Cassini*, the craft that confirmed the hexagon on Saturn, also recorded emissions from Saturn's magnetic field. Scientists have since turned them into audio waves. They're very similar to Earth's radio waves, and it's believed they're related to the auroras near Saturn's poles. It's a very exciting and interesting find, of course, but they still have no idea exactly where or what the emissions are coming from. They've coined them *the music of the spheres*. Like any other planet, Saturn is alive, and it's talking to us. Some might say seducing us. From Saturn's lips to our ears, eh?"

"This is all large and sweeping," I said. "How does any of this relate to what's happened to me? The people I encountered are all a bunch of lowlifes drugging unsuspecting saps like me so they can rob us of a few hundred bucks, not some power elite pulling the strings in some cosmic war of good and evil."

"Frontline flunkies," he said, dismissing me with another wave of his hand. "There are clubs and meeting houses and secret societies like that all over the world, most of them out in plain sight just like that one. No one cares, no one takes it seriously and no one knows what it's really all about or what it stands for. The people you encountered are foot soldiers and fools who think they're part of some larger, darker whole. And perhaps they are. Reality is subjective, Mr. Falk, much like time."

"And this drug they used on me, The Devil's Breath?"

"Control. They've done what they always do. They've handed it down

the ladder to those at the bottom to use on the rest of us like guinea pigs."
I must have struck him as unconvinced because he continued. "When
the CIA wanted to test a biological weapon, a form of virus they made in
a test tube, they had an operative drop a glass container of it on the sub-
way tracks in New York City. Then they sat back and waited to see what
happened, how many got sick, how long it took, how effective it was, and
if any died. The powerful have never been reluctant to experiment on the
weak, Mr. Falk. They do it every day. Imagine a drug as powerful as The
Devil's Breath that's been engineered to be even stronger than the one
they used on, as you say, a poor sap like you. What better way to get it out
into the population and see how it works when thrown as part of a much
larger net? Imagine if they could drop such chemicals from planes, let's
say, or add it in some form to our food or water, what then? And do you
for an instant believe they wouldn't do such a thing? Why wouldn't they?
No one would believe it anyway. Shadows, Mr. Falk, myth, they're very
powerful. That which cannot exist is free to do as it pleases. Meanwhile,
the dragon's games are getting worse. They believe this is their time, a
time they've worked for and those before them worked for, a time when
the gate will be opened and like good little lambs we will all shuffle off
to slaughter while they rule what's left, all of it theirs, beneath the rule
of their lord and master, the one to whom this all belongs. That's what
you're dealing with, Mr. Falk, whether you want it to be or believe it to
be or not. That is the reality no one wants to talk about or think about
because it's just too scary, just too disruptive and crazy. So the rest run
along and play with their cell phones and toys and gadgets, drowning in
their distractions while the world burns."

My mind spinning, I stood up, unable to sit still any longer. "What do
I do? How do I stop this?"

"You don't."

"What then? They're following me, they—"

"Once they know you're aware of them, they never completely let
you go."

"How do I get out of this then?"

"You run."

"Never been much of a runner."

"There is no fighting them."

"You do, you're still fighting, still trying to spread the truth."

"And look what they've done to me. No one's listening, Mr. Falk. I'm babbling to derelicts and mental defectives, present company excluded, of course. Make no mistake, they *will* destroy your life just like they did mine and countless others over the years. Or they'll eliminate you. Whatever they conclude is the easiest path, that's the one they'll take. Regardless, understand that you mean nothing to them. You and I and the rest of us, we're merely fleas on the back of a dog."

"It's hopeless then, that's what you're telling me?"

"You either run, or you go back to sleep. That's what I'm telling you."

"They're not going to let me sleep."

"It's not sleep you have to worry about. It's waking up."

"You talked about blood sacrifices. They still have these practices today?"

"Rituals," he said. "Everything they do has a purpose, a point. It's through the blood—the death, the ritual—that their power grows, Man's resolve weakens and the gateway moves closer to finally opening. You have to try to wrap your mind around things that are in direct conflict with what you've been taught. Virtually everything you know is a lie. Reality and time are not linear, as we've been led to believe. Time appears to be, yes? It seems as though we're born, live our lives, die, then move on to what awaits us, all in a straight line. That's an illusion. Time is not linear. Just like those clouds on Saturn, it's constantly spinning, blurring the boundaries between what we think is real and what we hope is not."

Never before had I felt quite so limited. "I don't understand."

"Do you know what space-time is?"

"Not really."

"It's any mathematical model that combines space and time into a single measurement, or continuum. The hexagon is space-time. There's something called a Planck length, which is the smallest piece of spacetime that can be observed, or exist relative to us. If one draws space-time, one must make all points one or whole multiples of one Planck length away from all others. Doing so creates a grid-like structure of space-time. This diagram is the only way that spacetime can be drawn, and because there are no fractions, the shape that arises is a two-dimensional hexagon that interacts with other hexagons. In turn, this creates larger and larger hexagons. If one views it three-dimensionally, one will see it automatically creates three-dimensional cubes, and those cubes create larger and larger cubes. This is why Einstein described space-time as having a grid-like structure. In the middle of that grid, were it to vibrate at the speed of light, the points connected to it would also vibrate. Those vibrations would continue outward and collide with each other head-on at specific points. This is where the speed of light squared comes from in Einstein's $E=MC^2$. Odds are, this is what a time machine would look like, a hexagon. In theory, it would warp space-time, making time travel possible." There was more movement behind him, this time what appeared to be several people shuffling into the darkness deeper in the tunnel. "What if this grid was all around us? What if our reality exists within that grid, the way a computer program exists within a larger framework? Then reality would not be what we perceive it to be. And time would cease to exist in the manner in which we believe it does. It would no longer be linear, but in a constant state of flux."

"This is..."

"Crazy? I told you that in the beginning. You need to separate madness from fallacy, do you understand? Your bits and pieces of memories of the night they drugged you are crazy, but that doesn't necessarily mean they're not true."

"I can't remember everything," I told him. "But they did more than rob me, they took me somewhere. I only have flashes of memories but it was somewhere horrible, and I think they killed someone. I heard screams, a woman in agony."

"Do you remember anything else?"

"There were signs, symbols, crude drawings on the walls."

"Describe them."

"I know now they were of Saturn on his throne, surrounded by ancient symbols for crosses. And there were...spiders..."

"Spiders?"

"Thousands of them on the ceiling. Not drawings, real spiders, moving like a single animal. If that really happened, if it was real, why did they let me go?"

For the first time, he said nothing.

"Tell me," I pressed. "Why would they let me go?"

The Professor stood, moved over to the opposite wall and a series of small overturned crates he used as a makeshift desk, and shuffled through some papers. I could tell he was bluffing. There was nothing there he needed to see, he just didn't want to look me in the eye.

He remained where he was, his back to me.

"Professor, *why*? Why would they let me go?"

"They wouldn't," he said softly.

"Then why did they?"

He finally faced me, his eyes alive with sorrow. "Maybe they didn't."

I got up. There seemed nothing else to say, no response that made any sense. The world was melting like a wax sculpture, and me along with it.

"In my cottage," I said a moment later, "they performed a ritual, left a talisman and things painted on the walls."

"Do you have a family?"

"No."

"A career you care about?"

"I wash dishes."

"Is there anything tying you to this area or the life you lead here?"

"Nothing."

"Then go home. Pack a bag and leave. Tell no one. Start over somewhere else and hope they leave you alone."

"Where the hell am I supposed to go?"

"Anywhere far from here."

"I'm not sure it's that's easy."

"It isn't. There's a storm coming, Mr. Falk, a terrible storm the likes of which this world and everyone in it has never before experienced or even realized is possible. A storm no one will ever recover from. Regardless of what you or I or anyone else does, or believes or disbelieves or wants or desires, likes or dislikes, that storm is coming, and nothing short of divine intervention can stop it. The question is when. Go and live out your life as best you can, pretend none of this ever happened, and that none of what you now know is real. Otherwise this will slowly rot your mind and drive you completely insane. It will dominate your every thought and leave you whimpering beneath the blankets in your bed because it's all too much to handle, because the deeper you dig the more you'll find and the more fantastical it will become. Knowing what you know, how do you go on with your life like before? You don't, but you can try. You can try and hope and pray it—and they—leave you alone, and perhaps—just perhaps—you'll be allowed to fade away, because in the end, you don't matter anyway. None of us do. Look at me. Look at how I live."

"You don't think it's too late for all that?"

"It wasn't wise to go to that man's apartment in Brockton."

My heart began to race. "How did... How did you know that?"

"But there's still a chance," he said, ignoring me. "He didn't tell you anything that might lead you to anyone higher up and likely couldn't have even had he wanted to because he wasn't in possession of such information. They know that, so at this point there's nothing to tie you to anyone other than a handful of low-level hoodlums. From what you've told me, nothing you've done has touched those that matter yet, and that could very well be a saving grace."

"How did you know I'd been there?" I asked again.

The Professor considered me the way one might a befuddled child, but he wasn't condescending, I could tell he truly pitied me. Him, a man hiding and living underground, pitied me. "Time is not linear."

I nodded, though I still didn't know what he meant. "One thing he did tell me was that these rituals they hold take place at different locations every time and that even a lot of the people going don't know where or when they'll be until right before they do it."

"He was correct. Harder for anyone to track their activities that way."

"And how do you know for sure these gatherings really take place, that these rituals actually happen? How can you be sure it's not all rumor, a bunch of spook stories no one can ever prove?"

The Professor stroked his beard and sighed. "Because I've seen them."

"You've seen one of these gatherings where people were murdered?"

"Sacrificed."

"To Saturn."

It wasn't a question but he nodded anyway.

"You *saw* this happen?"

"Not the blood sacrifices, no."

"Then what are we talking about?"

He glanced into the darkness behind him, as if for permission. "While doing research for my book," he explained, "I was able to obtain enough information from an insider to allow me to briefly infiltrate one of their meetings. I saw enough."

"Who was this person?"

"He's of no use to you. He's dead."

"Because of what he told you?"

"I don't know."

"Where did the meeting take place?" I asked.

"Doesn't matter now, they'll never return there."

"But there's another one, isn't there? One soon. One here, in Sunset."

"This takes a part of you no one should ever have to give," he said quietly. "Pieces of you no one should ever have to lose. But the spider doesn't fear the fly."

"So I hear." I was losing my grip, my head spinning.

"The predator never expects to become the prey."

I knew then what he meant.

"Once the fire is extinguished," he told me, "they'll scurry away into the night like the cockroaches they are."

"And these alleged victims, no one ever goes looking for them?"

"People disappear every day. Children vanish by the thousands all over the country. If you stopped to look at the actual statistics, you'd be amazed, the numbers are quite sobering. Most of these people, even the children, no one really cares about or spends a lot of time looking for beyond all the initial hoopla and searches and proclamations. Few are ever found—dead or alive—or even heard from again."

"Time passes," I said.

"Precisely. People forget, stop caring. They move on."

"And this Brotherhood of Saturn are behind these sacrifices too?"

"A good deal of them, yes, but you must understand that those are the extremes, the blood rituals. Countless other rituals to Saturn are performed every day by people who have no idea they're involved in them at all. Are you married, Mr. Falk?"

"Not anymore."

"When you were, did you and your wife exchange and wear wedding rings?"

"Yes."

"Do you know why? Why rings and not something else? Ever wonder what the origin of that tradition is?"

I wasn't sure which bothered me more, his line of questioning or the fact that I'd never thought about or questioned something as commonplace as wedding rings.

"They represent the rings of Saturn," he said. "It's a way to honor him, a sign that he oversees and blesses the union. People do it to this day without knowing why, how it started, what it really means or to whom it truly pays tribute."

I looked at my hand, the finger where I'd once worn a gold ring.

"Did you know that in Mecca there's a big black stone cube they pray before called the Kaaba?" The Professor asked. "They move around it, simultaneously, as one, in this giant crowd, and when they do, the entire scene looks exactly like the clouds moving around the hexagon on the north pole of Saturn. They even move in the same direction, counterclockwise. There are countless comparative videos available online and elsewhere. And it doesn't stop there. Nearly every major religion so deeply worships Saturn that it's uncanny, and the most frightening part is virtually none of them know they're doing it. It's all deception."

"How did Duane know about you?" I asked. "About this?"

"He's a part of it."

"I don't understand, he—"

"We're *all* a part of it. You're no different than we are, no different than all the others out there wrapped up in this horror. Nothing is an accident. Nothing is coincidence or contrivance. It's all pieces to a larger puzzle, strands of a whole cloth, a play being performed by people unaware there's a play at all." He drifted closer to the darkness, until a hand appeared and pushed something into his palm, a small plastic bottle of prescription pills. He popped two, swallowed them dry, then handed the bottle back to those awaiting him in the dark. "Anxiety," he said sheepishly. "The pills help keep it at bay."

"Got to fight that dragon however we can," I said.

"Until the gateway opens, it's all we can do, live and die as our souls come and go, passing through the polarized rings of Saturn. That's where they go, you know, our souls. It's where our souls enter this dimension…and where they leave it."

"What good would that do if the gateway's closed?"

"We're not talking about the physical realm. That's why people miss what's all around them. It's like looking for oranges in an apple orchard, then claiming oranges are a lie since none can be found. Not only are they looking in the wrong place, they refuse to believe the right place exists even when it's pointed out to them. It results in a perfect storm of arrogant ignorance disguised as intellectual superiority. Meanwhile, the deception rages on."

"Then Heaven help us," I said.

"We're a long way from Heaven, Mr. Falk."

In that oddly surreal moment, bathed in flickering candlelight and waiting for his narcotics to kick in, Quinton Cassells looked not only like the sad and deeply troubled man he was, but someone drowning hopelessly in his own madness.

And as shadows gathered and drifted across his face in that horrible place deep underground, I could tell he saw the same things in me.

18

RAIN SPRAYED THE JETTY, mixing with the crashing waves. Duane stood on the rocks seemingly unaffected, staring out at the dark horizon. I stayed behind him, on the sand, watching his tattered clothes blowing in the wind.

"Shit gets in your head," he said. "Fucks with you."

"Can't get it out. Just seems to get worse."

"Look at the skies," he said. "They never used to look like that."

I did, and he was right.

Devil's breathing all over you, baby.

"We're all gonna die, aren't we, Duane?"

He partially looked back, but not far enough to make eye contact, then returned his gaze to the ocean. "Of course."

Night had begun to fall, and the worst of the storm had yet to arrive. But just like the encroaching darkness, it was coming, and with a vengeance. For me it was all about going back. I knew that now. Back into what I'd just narrowly escaped.

"You should go home," Duane said.

"Not yet." The ocean air and its chilly spray felt good against my flushed skin.

"A man should always go home when he can."

"If I do…*when* I do…who's going to be there?"

This time when Duane turned, he looked right at me. "What happened to your face?"

I backed away, slowly at first, and then I was running, throwing myself into the wind and stumbling forward, pushing hard as I could, going fast as my body and the sand at my feet would allow. With countless nightmarish scenarios turning over and over again in my mind, I eventually reached the base of the dunes leading to my cottage. Above, a light burned in the back windows. There was something hypnotic about the glow of light burning through the darkness.

I stood there in the rain, unable to move, unable to look away.

Whispers…muddled laughter…the sound of waves crashing ashore…

I dropped to my knees. There was someone in the window, a silhouette looking down at the beach, motionless and waiting, but for what?

For you, Stan…

The world began to tilt and spin. I closed my eyes, felt myself toppling over into the sand. It was cool and moist against my face, and the rain felt good in my hair and running down along the back of my neck. But I was afraid because I knew I was not alone. There was someone else here; someone behind me on the beach, and it wasn't Duane. It wasn't even the same beach.

When I opened my eyes, I was lying on my belly like a commando. A dull headache pulsed at the base of my skull as I struggled back to my feet and groggily looked around.

I could smell the remnants of a fire mixed with those of the ocean. All around me, tall grass swayed in the darkness, bending to and fro in the wind and rain. Below the dunes beyond it, I could see where the bonfire had been, where they'd taken us, and I realized then it was possible we'd never left. Yet it all seemed so very long ago somehow, an event that existed in a whirlwind where nightmare and memory were one.

Time no longer made sense. Maybe it never had.

I came to a stop at the summit of the dunes, still trying to understand how I'd gotten here or what was happening. Great pillars of black smoke rose from the dead bonfire, separating from the darkness and gracefully drifting through the night. Billowing in thick tumbling plumes, the smoke reached for the blue-black sky, where it was absorbed back into night, an exhale of death, gone but still alive, hidden in its cloak of darkness.

And there, down on the deserted beach, a lone figure waited for me on the far side of where the fire had been.

I descended the dunes and trudged across the sand until I'd reached the burned-out pit that had once been a bonfire. Steam still rose from it, mixing with the pouring rain. Across from me stood the blonde woman. Nude now, she smiled through the mist, smoke and darkness, her brilliantly white teeth cutting the night, more sinister and feral than beautiful.

Quickly, I scanned the immediate area as best I could. If there were still others here, they were extremely well hidden. I returned to the woman's glazed eyes, her wild short blonde hair and petite body covered in numerous black tattoos—more symbols and talismans bold against her pale skin—and prepared myself for what I might have to do. I reached around to the back of my pants, pulled the gun free and let my arm hang at my side.

She ran toward the water, spinning and skipping, her arms out on either side of her, head thrown back in ecstasy. But she made no sound, even when I followed her. Instead, she stopped short of the waves and spun back to me, her naked white flesh piercing the night.

With that bright grin in place, the woman spun closer, her diminutive breasts shaking, the dark pink nipples small but long, taut and hard. Completely shaved, a large tattoo of an ankh decorated her lower belly, positioned to look as if it had been stabbed into her vagina and was emerging directly from between her legs.

Still, she said nothing and made no sound. She reached for me, motioning me to come to her, to let her embrace me, but I stayed where I was, the gun still down by my side.

She continued to motion, seductively running her hands across her body, which was slick and wet from the rain. Her hair was plastered against her face, and the black eye makeup and bright red lipstick she'd sported earlier had all but washed away. She moved closer, her little bare feet tiptoeing closer as she pranced across the sand like an imp.

I held my ground but turned slightly to the side, to shield my gun hand. The woman stopped a few feet from me, but was so close I could see the veins in her eyes and the beads of rain dripping from her hair. Again, she motioned for me to fall into her embrace.

My resolve was weakening.

"Take me to them," I said. "Take me to the others."

She gave a childlike gleeful nod and reached for me, her fingertips brushing my arm, just barely touching it. A chill slithered through me. I slid the gun back into my pants and leaned closer, allowing her fingers to close over my arm this time and pull me to her.

I fell against her and dropped to my knees. She was short, so even though she was standing, my head was in line with the center of her chest. I shivered as fear, confusion and primal lust merged. I didn't want her anywhere near me, didn't want her touching me and I didn't want to touch her. But I couldn't stop myself.

Her hands clutched either side of my head and crushed my face into her breasts, grinding me rhythmically against her until I took one of her nipples into my mouth. Her chest heaved as I suckled it, tasted rain and salt and then something else, something metallic. My hands slid around her waist, then down onto her ass, cupping and squeezing it, pulling her closer still.

Something more than rain sprayed my face, and the same metallic taste on my tongue grew worse. I turned my head and her breast was released from my mouth with a loud pop. Gagging, I spit out a mouthful of blood. Her blood.

I scrambled back, watched as the woman cupped her breasts and squeezed them together, blood spraying from them in fine streams across her belly and onto the fronts of her thighs. But there were no wounds, no visible injuries. The blood was being secreted directly from her breasts as she milked them and laughed silently, her eyes wild and demonic.

Frantically wiping my mouth with the back of my hand, I got back to my feet in time to see someone moving down by the water. A man, emerging from the surf as if born from it, walked unsteadily toward shore.

The side of his head was missing, blown away. And then I knew who he was.

When he'd been alive.

He looked at me, opened his mouth to speak, but instead vomited thick black blood that gushed out over his lips and down the front of him.

A huge wave crashed ashore, and the man vanished into it. When the wave was gone, so was he.

But the woman remained.

She ran into the darkness.

I followed.

19

IN THE DARKNESS AND rain, all I could see was her stark white backside moving through the night in front of me. Under more normal circumstances, it might've seemed comical or even erotic, but on this night it was just another example of a world gone mad, where nothing made sense or was what it appeared to be.

By the time the woman ran past a sign posted on the sand that declared the beach beyond that point to be private property, my lungs were burning and my muscles were so sore and weak I could barely stand. Exhausted, I dropped to my hands and knees with the hope of catching my breath. Soaking wet, I wiped rain from my eyes, read the sign a second time, then looked to the stretch of beach where the woman waited for me. A handful of beautiful homes sat perched above us, built into the hills and cliffs overlooking the sand. We'd gone so far we'd reached the wealthiest section of Sunset. I'd never been there before.

I struggled to my feet and followed the woman until I'd reached a series of steps built into the side of the hills, complete with railings and torches lining either side of them all the way up to the mansion above. The torches were unlit in the storm, but I imagined what they might look like on any other night, burning majestically and showing the way to whatever alleged Shangri-la those who lived there had created.

To my left, lightning stabbed the night in giant spears, bathing the area in a flash of blue before returning us to darkness. In that split second, I saw that the woman was standing on the bottom step, smiling at me maniacally.

My legs were weak and I wanted nothing more than to fall again to my knees, but I instead staggered over to her, stopping just short of the step. She opened her arms and threw back her head, looking as if she were laughing but making no sound.

Above us, at the top of those steps, there were others. I could see them now, in their dark hooded robes, little more than shadows and silhouettes standing in the rain, watching us. And then, in unison, they raised their heads to reveal striking white masks, eyeholes cut into them but otherwise smooth as porcelain.

Like pieces of a larger whole, I thought, *a larger, fully realized organism.*

Through the storm, I could hear the faintest sounds of chanting, prayers muttered and riding the wind as the robed figures moved together, swaying like the tall grass along the dunes.

Moving as one, I thought, *just like the spiders.*

The blonde woman suddenly lunged at me and took my face in her small, cold hands. "We do not react to what happens in this world," she said in a singsong voice. "This world reacts to what happens in *us.* Born in blood, you die and are reborn in fire. This is your crucible. Kill for us. Kill for *him.* You hunger. Let him feed you."

A fist slammed into the side of my head, connecting with my temple and the upper part of my ear. The blow threw my equilibrium off and set the world on a slow-moving perpetual tilt. Falling sideways, then forward, I threw my hands out in an attempt to break the fall, but I'd already landed, crashing to the sand chin-first. Pain burst from behind my eyes and out of my mouth as I bit down and my teeth came together with a sickening clacking sound.

The next thing I knew I was instinctively trying to stand, pushing myself up onto all fours and looking around, struggling to focus. Those circling me appeared as little more than a blur of colors, vague shapes along with everything else in my line of sight. A wave of panic surged through me as my vision slowly began to come back into focus. I fell back onto my ass and tasted blood. Though I blinked rapidly and repeatedly, everything remained encased in a blurry film. It was like looking through a lens smeared with Vaseline.

Three figures moved closer to me, my vision correcting enough for me to see that it was Braids, Teddy and his other bald flunky.

I tried to stand, but Braids put a boot against my chest and pushed me back, pinning me to the sand, his piercing blue eyes staring down at me.

When I struggled, he slid his foot to my throat, so I gripped his leg with both hands and swept my leg hard as I could. Connecting with his ankle, it knocked his leg out from under him and sent him sprawling.

Teddy closed on me as I pushed myself to my feet. Just in time, I crossed my arms over my face, blocking his incoming punch, then fired back with a combination to his liver that dropped him. Hitting a man in the liver was the same as kicking out his knee or kneeing him in the testicles. Made no difference what kind of shape you were in or how tough you were, you get hit there hard enough, down you go.

I staggered away, jumping over Braids, who was already scrambling to his feet, and yanked the gun from the back of my pants. But before I could level it, Braids swung at me, knocking the gun from my hand. It flew away as the force of the blow knocked me off balance as well. I stumbled back, braced myself, and threw a three-punch combination at him.

With the skill of a seasoned boxer, he dodged the first two. The third clipped his cheek but just grazed him, and he walked right through it, throwing a solid uppercut into my gut that forced all the air out of me in a single gasp.

As I doubled over, he grabbed hold of me by my collar and, like a bouncer, threw me several feet into the air. I landed and rolled through the fall as best I could. Sore, out of breath and still light-headed, I managed to stand before Braids reached me, but he was closing quickly, a look of steely determination on his face. I glanced around for something to fight him off with.

He hit me before I could get out of the way. Momentum sent me flying, and I landed on my back. I lay there a moment, trying to catch my breath, the rain pouring down on me.

I rolled over and stood up just in time to see all three men coming at me. Braids moved to the side as Teddy came at me first, so I stood and grabbed the nearest thing I could, a gnarled piece of driftwood partially buried in the sand. Picking it up and swinging it all in one fluid motion, it cracked him full in the face. Blood sprayed us both as he stumbled back. I came back around with it and hit him again, this time on the side of his head. He dropped to his knees and fell over in an unconscious heap.

The third man charged. He was focused on the weapon in my hands, so I threw a quick front-kick to his knee, which badly hyperextended, then buckled it with a savage snapping sound. Clutching his leg, he fell to the sand, wailing in agony.

I circled him. Keeping an eye on Braids, who was watching but not yet charging me, I stomped my heel down into the man's throat, crushing his windpipe.

By the time I'd readied my stance, my eyes still on Braids, the man had gagged and choked into unconsciousness. A moment or two later, he was dead.

Braids casually shrugged off the vest he was wearing and assumed a fighting stance. Shirtless and showcasing his impressive physique, he came at me suddenly, and with more speed than seemed possible, threw an elbow that missed, followed by a spinning back-kick that whizzed by my head like a bullet, missing me by inches.

I countered with a kick to his knee, but despite his bulk, he was too agile, and slid out of the way before I could connect, coming back around with a forearm that connected with my jaw and took me off my feet.

I fell, the air gone from me again as I kicked and convulsed like a fish out of water. Coughing, I rolled onto my knees and tried to get up, but he was on me again, this time raining a fist down across my face that should've put me down for good.

Lying on my side, everything blurred then cleared, blurred then cleared again, and a loud ringing in my ears slowly subsided until sound returned like a radio gradually increasing in volume.

The rain just kept coming, soaking us down.

Braids flexed his muscles and circled me like a jungle cat.

"Get up," he growled.

I struggled onto my knees, unsure if I could even stand at that point. I tried, failed, and as I rolled over, realized I'd landed on the gun. It was wedged against the small of my back. I pulled it free, fell back and fired.

The first shot hit Braids in the throat. The second shot exploded his left eye.

The third missed, as he'd already fallen, dead before he hit the ground.

With an eerie calmness I didn't quite understand, I stood and walked over to Teddy. He was still lying there unconscious.

I shot him twice in the back of the head.

I stood there a moment, breathing slowly and deliberately.

Perched on the first step leading to the house and the others was Felix, staring at me through the rain with a demonic sparkle in his black eyes.

"Do it," he said, slowly rising to his feet, arms held out on either side of him in mock crucifixion.

You'll pray to us one day.

My sins, my guilt, my weakness and horror, it was all there with me. And the Devil, he was there too, his tail slithering up between my legs, his talons taking me by the hand, assuring me everything would be all right.

"Do it!" Hell's saint shouted above the storm.

I looked Felix dead in the eye. Then I shot him in the face.

He fell back and away into darkness in an explosion of blood and rain, as I stumbled away and dropped the gun.

The blonde woman appeared out of the darkness.

The demented prayers of those watching grew louder.

Her face contorted, hideously distorted in the rain and madness. The same face I'd seen before, exploding from the darkness, a demon— a witch—blowing into her open palm and dispersing a cloud of mist that sprayed my face.

And suddenly we were falling back, together. We landed in the wet sand with her on top of me, her nude body slick as she writhed about, hands still clutching my face. I tried in vain to grip her tiny waist, but my hands slid free, up over the small of her back and onto her buttocks.

I wanted her off me. I wanted to get up. I wanted to get away from this place. But I could accomplish none of those things. Instead, I lay there, blinking rapidly and trying to see through the rain to those robed figures watching from above, but I'd lost them in the storm. All I could see was a forest of impossibly white shiny faces sprinkled across the hills like the bad dream they were, detached and no longer human, faces without noses or mouths, just empty, black, lifeless eyes.

The woman was grinding on me, and my body was responding, hardening beneath her as she slammed her pelvis down against mine again and again, her hands holding my face with such passion it now felt as if her fingers would push their way through my flesh at any moment, puncturing it so she could reach inside me with those delicate fingers. Her lips brushed mine and her tongue flickered about like a snake's, pushing against my mouth until it found its way inside.

We rolled, and I was on top of her, holding her small frame tight against me as I kissed her harder, meeting her thrusts with my own as she fumbled with my pants, yanking them down, freeing me of them. I knew they were there, the others, watching and saying their horrible prayers, but I couldn't stop. Her hands slid free of my face, gripping my cock instead, guiding it closer as her legs wrapped around my lower back.

The rain continued to fall, and the storm raged on as I entered her.

Slamming into her, my hands found her tender throat, latched on and squeezed as I fucked her harder and harder, smashing her petite body deeper into the wet sand. I could hear her muffled cries turn to gagging as I strangled the life from her, but I kept on, fucking her with savage thrusts before finally letting go of her throat. I postured up over her, felt my hand tighten into a fist. I cocked it back, ready to pummel her beautiful face with it, to annihilate it with my knuckles. And as her eyes widened and blood trickled from her mouth, she smiled and bucked against my erection, forcing me deeper inside her.

But through the rain it all blurred and became something else, and all I could see was my pitiful old man, and how I'd dreamt of beating his face in with these same fists. How I'd fantasized so many times of hurting him the same way he'd hurt my mother, the same way he'd hurt me. How many people had I beaten and tortured for money, every time pretending it was my father instead? Could I even remember? Was there a number that might somehow give it all some sense, that might somehow justify my violence and depravity, my rage against those who had done nothing to me?

The prayers were louder now, swirling around us like the wind and rain, making it all worse. Darker…blacker…more horrific somehow…

The woman smiled, showing her bright white teeth, now smeared with blood and spittle.

I brought my fist down into her face and fucked her until the rain and wetness from between her legs exploded as one against us, spraying up over our bellies and chests. I hit her again, harder this time, and kept fucking her even though all that splashed between us had turned to blood. Her blood. My blood.

And then she was gone. The face no longer hers, no longer my father's, but someone else's, and my rage and senseless violence turned to shame. I slammed shut my eyes and fell away to the beach, rolling away and pushing my face down into the wet sand, hoping it might smother me and put an end to this horror.

Daddy?

"No! Goddamn it, no!"

Don't be sad, Daddy.

Little fingers reached down into the sand, found my eyes, gently wiped the tears from them, then found the sockets and pushed, stabbing slowly, deeply. Agonizing pain fired through my skull as her fingers punctured my eyeballs with a hideous popping sound.

"Stop, please—you—you're killing me!"

A soupy froth bubbled and bled from the holes where my eyes had been.

What happened to your face?

I fell forward, collapsing onto the woman, her face buried against my neck, my lips pressed to her face, tasting her blood as it ran into my mouth and down my throat, coating it with a sickening metallic flavor that was at once nauseating and seductive, so primal and raw and infectious.

Come and see, Daddy. Come and see.

Above the sounds of our labored breath and the rapid beat of her heart, I again heard the prayers of the others, even more clearly now, above the din of the storm.

Come and see.

And I saw.

* * *

The king watches from his throne, the wall around him stained in blood and gore, the ceiling above coated in spiders.

My head spins, feels as if it's loose from the rest of my body and floating away across the room, flying above the bones and blood, dampness and cold. But as I try to stand and fail, my face slaps the tiled floor and reminds me I am not free to fly away at all, but tethered to this horror, and it to me.

It's gotten dark. I can see night creeping in through the blown-out window, the darkness swallowing the fog, devouring it the same way the madness is devouring me, eating me from the inside out like the ravenous parasite it is.

Someone comes, moving down a long and dark hallway toward the room. I cannot see who it is, but I can see black boots moving closer through the darkness, and then suddenly this person has hold of me by the ankle and I'm spinning around and being effortlessly dragged across the floor like a carcass, my chest, stomach, face and hands sliding across the bloody, bone-littered floor as above, the spiders come awake.

They begin to fall.

The last thing I see is Saturn atop his throne, surrounded by his bloody symbols, and the giant pentagram painted in blood along the floor.

Into the darkness, I'm dragged along a dirty, cracked and horribly pitted floor. I want to kick out at the person dragging me with my other foot, but my leg dangles there lifelessly, refusing to cooperate. I cannot get my body to do anything my mind screams for it to do, my protests nothing more than muffled whimpers.

We reach another room, this one darker and windowless, with a series of candles burning and positioned in a large circle along the floor. My leg is released.

I push myself groggily onto my side, look around frantically.

The candlelight licks the dark walls, reflects off the tile floors. The man that dragged me here, a hulking shadow, disappears back down the hallway without ever uttering a word.

It isn't until I hear the rattling of chains that I realize I'm not alone in the room. There is someone else here, in the far corner, just beyond the reach of flames.

I crawl closer to the circle of candles, and in doing so gain a better look into the dark corner. Someone slight, I cannot tell if the figure is male or female, is nude and huddled there, manacles about the wrists and ankles.

The figure is chained to the wall.

"Please," the shadow says, and I know then it's a woman. "Don't."

A sudden intrusion of greater fire sprays and explodes on the other side of the room, revealing a bevy of robed figures standing in an even larger circle that surrounds us. All wear the unsettling white porcelain-like masks and black satin hooded robes, save for three, who are clad in red robes and wear masks of gold.

An odd melody emanates from the circle. Eerie and dripping with melancholy, it echoes off the walls and down the dark hallway, a strange sound reminiscent of monks singing from the depths of some ancient stone temple, their voices at once ethereal, menacing and strangely beautiful. The words are from some long-dead language I cannot understand.

I bring my hands to my face, trace the slashed flesh along my cheeks and chin with bloody fingers and try to understand what's happening to me.

Above us there is no longer a roof, just a large, jagged, long-destroyed fissure, a portal to a vast, star-filled canopy of night.

A ball of fire separates from the stars, drifting and burning overhead as it turns the darkness to light.

No. Not light, something similar to light.

A horrible screech rings in my ears, stabs into my temples and pushes at the backs of my eyes as my stomach spasms and burns, threatening to violently empty its contents at any moment. I'm sure I'll die if it continues, but I don't know how to make it stop. I don't know what to do.

I look to the others as the night sky burns.

In response, one of the red robes nods his face of gold.

I hear a voice inside my head that is not my own.

"Feed," it says. "Feed."

And I do.

*   *   *

Lights moved along the far wall, slipping away like ghosts before I could figure out exactly what had caused them. My vision, though blurred, focused enough for me to see the small dark room around me. Gone was the blood and horror. It was quiet here, and comfortable, as I'd been put to bed and covered with heavy, luxurious sheets and blankets. The lush pillows beneath my head smelled vaguely of lavender, and on the nightstand to my left a stick of incense slowly burned in a small gold holder. I watched the thin tendrils of smoke spiral into the air, the oddly seductive smell it produced wafting around me.

I tried to move but my body was tender, stiff and so weak I couldn't even raise my head from the pillows or reach up and scratch my nose. Whenever I swallowed, I tasted traces of blood, which left me nauseated, and although the horrible migraine was gone, the base of my skull still pulsed with dull and steady pain. I ran my tongue across my teeth and gums. They were sore and coated with a sour film. I wanted to get up, to call out, but instead, I felt myself drifting away, back into the darkness from which I'd just emerged.

This process repeated itself numerous times, I can't say how many or for how long, because I lost all sense of time and place and self, collapsed and drifting in and out of consciousness. But at some point, I came awake in the same bed and this time felt more alert and focused, more in control of my mind and body.

I lay there a while, watching the ceiling.

No spiders, only shadows.

The door slowly opened.

An older balding man stepped inside. Dressed in a dated black suit, he moved cautiously, as if to make as little noise as possible, his hands folded before him as he leaned closer for a better look at me.

"You're awake," he said in a soft, pleasant voice that seemed in conflict with his intense, birdlike features. "How are you feeling, sir?"

I tried to speak but only managed a guttural croaking sound.

"Just a moment." The man hurried into the shadows on the far side of the room and returned with a carafe of water and a small glass. He poured the water, set the carafe on the nightstand and lowered the glass to my lips, placing his other hand gently behind my neck and lifting my head until my mouth met the glass and I could take a drink. "There you are, sir," he said, taking it away and laying my head back into the pillows after only a second or two. "Not too much at first, your stomach's probably already upset as it is."

The water was lukewarm but felt good. I hadn't realized how parched I was until I swallowed and felt my tongue and mouth hydrate back to life. I licked my lips, moistening the cracked, chapped skin.

The man placed the glass on the nightstand and straightened his posture, cocking his head as he gazed down at me. "Better?"

I nodded, swallowed. "Where am I?" I asked, my voice raspy, throat sore.

"We found you on the beach," the man said. "You were quite ill."

"The woman…"

"Woman, sir?"

"The blonde woman that was with me."

"There was no woman, sir. Only you. Apparently you became disoriented during the storm and collapsed at the base of the stairs leading to the house. We didn't know what was wrong, exactly, but we brought you in and put you to bed. Luckily one of the neighbors is a doctor, and he came and saw you the other night. We've been giving you the antibiotics and sleeping aids he prescribed as you had a very high fever when we found you. We couldn't be sure what had happened, but there seemed no reason to phone the police. Dr. Pascuiles felt you'd be good as new in a few days."

"How long have I been here?"

"Nearly three days, Mr. Falk."

I squinted in the hope of bringing him into clearer focus. "How do you know my name?"

"Your wallet was in your pants, sir. We found your ID."

"Have you contacted anyone?"

"I'm afraid we really had no idea who to get ahold of. We were unable to find a partner, next of kin, anyone associated with you or much information about you at all, frankly, so we thought it best to just let you rest and recover and address all that at a later time."

I tried to sit up, and was able to, partially, but I was still horribly weak. "Who are you?"

"Argus Peacock, sir." He extended his hand. "Pleasure."

I managed to lift my arm enough to take his hand in mine. His flesh was warm and smooth, his grip genteel. "Is this your house?"

"Oh, heavens, no." Argus laughed politely. "I only work here, watching over the place, and Mr. Buck, of course."

I fought sleep, but it was coming for me again and there seemed little I could do to stop it. "I want to see him, I—I want to talk to *Mr. Buck*."

"Of course, sir. All in good time." Argus smiled, revealing long, narrow teeth faded a dull yellow. "But for now, it's best you rest and regain your strength. When you're feeling better, we'll get this all worked out. For now, I assure you, you're in good hands and under my personal watchful eye, Mr. Falk."

The rest started to come back to me in flashes. I wanted out. Now.

"Easy, sir," Argus said, gently placing a liver-spotted hand on my shoulder.

"I know who you are," I said, struggling to find the strength to drag myself from the bed. "I know what you are, I—I—"

"Don't upset yourself," Argus said. "Everything will be all right, sir."

Hard as I fought it, my eyes grew impossibly heavy, slowly slid shut, and despite my panic, I slipped off to sleep once again.

20

MY DREAMS HAVE ALWAYS *been haunted. I'm afraid of them, lucid or otherwise, because I know they are more than nightmares conjured in an exhausted and battered mind. They are keepsakes, souvenirs from the horrible things within me that nest and thrive, slowly growing and feeding off me even as I tell myself they're all in the past, tidily forgotten and packed away like old toys no longer played with.*

The nature of all beasts changes at any given moment, but the beast itself remains. After all, it is not we who react to this world, but this world that reacts to us. Our world is haunted because we are haunted. By deed and thought, memory and cognition, we are damned or saved.

We move in light but dream in darkness. Spiders all, we are unafraid of the fly, fearful instead of our own kind, our other, *not that which we kill but that which we give life, as that is what will devour us just as surely as we devour the fly.*

It's a terrible thing to know terrible things.

Come and see…

As I move through the door and step beneath the rainbow, I see they're all here, gathered as if for some greater good, a charity cocktail party in Hell.

They all stop and look at me, and for a moment, I freeze. Then, apparently satisfied with my presence, they return to their conversations, resume whatever they were doing when I arrived.

Colors melt and blend together, sight and sound and smell not quite right in this fever dream, this voyage of lucid horror flickering like a flame at the very edges of my sanity, or whatever resides there now in its place.

I stand there stupidly, trying to understand.

Across the room, Albert is doing one of his martial arts routines while Carla and some others watch. They both see me and smile. I look away, only to find Duane standing alone in the corner, dressed in his filthy rags, a glass in hand. Ashamed, he refuses to make eye contact.

Slide sits in a chair nearby, softly strumming a guitar balanced on his knee. He looks up and winks at me. Standing nearby and swaying slowly in time with his tune is Ginny-Anne, the bank manager. She grins, points at me playfully.

The Professor stands before a set of double windows on the back wall, gazing out at a horizon in flames. I try to focus on the fire reflected in his eyes rather than the young boys on their knees encircling him, and a handful of partygoers watching the children's hideous efforts with demonic glee.

We've all been deceived, Mr. Falk.

The others I don't recognize and don't believe I have ever seen before. Yet there is something familiar about them, something I recognize in them. We are kindred spirits, all of us.

One day you'll pray to us.

My vision blurs through what can only be tears as another person separates from a cluster of partygoers, approaches and hands me a glass of the thick red liquid.

Something moves between my legs. I look down.

Balthazar, his serpentine movements between my calves oddly fascinating as he slinks about, stopping occasionally to rub his head against me and purr loudly.

I look up into Sophie's eyes.

"It's okay," she says, pushing the glass at me. "Take it."

I close my eyes. If only someone would sew them shut and make all this go away. But it doesn't go away. It survives. In the dark. With me.

When I open my eyes, Sophie is still there, holding that awful drink out for me, but something else catches my attention.

The blonde woman is leaning against the wall to my right. Still nude, battered and bloody, she clutches an oval mirror to her chest. I have seen that mirror before. I have seen what lives inside it.

Laughing silently, she slowly walks up the wall and across the ceiling.

Across the room, a man in a black suit stands in the corner, facing the wall. As if aware that I've noticed him, he very slowly turns around.

His eyes. My God, his eyes, dozens of them scattered impossibly across his face, blinking in unison, staring at me with their dead gaze.

Argus Peacock's watchful eyes...

My mind splinters, dissolves away with all the rest in dust devils of screams and horrible, joyless laughter.

* * *

I awakened to the sound of chanting. More singing, really, and piped in at a low volume through speakers built invisibly into the walls, it possessed a haunting quality that made me uneasy.

This time I was able to sit up easily, my strength returned to me. I pushed away the blankets and swung my feet around to the floor. Dressed in a pair of red silk pajamas, my feet bare, I stood. My head spun a bit but quickly righted itself, and I was able to cross the room to a chair in the corner where my clothes were laid out. They'd been washed, pressed and neatly folded. Having spent the last however many hours sweating and feverish, I smelled and needed a shower, but my only thought just then was to get dressed and get the hell out of whatever this place was.

I had just finished dressing when someone knocked lightly on the door. I didn't respond but the door opened anyway, and Argus Peacock stepped in, his face no longer the multi-eyed monstrosity from my nightmares.

"You're up and about," he said pleasantly. "Obviously feeling much better, splendid! And I've more good news, sir. Mr. Buck is available to see you, if you'd still like to speak with him, that is."

"Take me to him," I said, my throat still sore but my voice more like my own.

"Of course, sir." He pointed to an adjacent bathroom I hadn't noticed previously. "If you'd like to freshen up first, I've taken the liberty of providing you with a fresh toothbrush, some soap and shaving materials."

I hesitated, unsure of what to do.

"Go ahead, sir," Peacock said, retreating. "I'll wait for you in the hallway."

The bathroom was beautiful, like something in a high-end hotel.

I ran the water, washed my face and hands, then brushed my teeth and straightened my hair. I didn't shave, although I was in bad need of one, but was mesmerized by the straight razor on the counter, its silver blade reflecting the light with ominous beauty. Visions of it running across my wrists and then face flashed in my mind, forcing me to look at my reflection in the mirror once again.

Deep scars crisscrossed my cheeks. I brought a shaking hand to my face, ran my fingers along the canals carved into my flesh. They felt old, as if I'd had them for years. I looked down, grabbed the sink with both hands and steadied myself.

What have you done to me?

My fury building, I found Argus just outside the bedroom door. With a smile he motioned for me to follow him and started down a long carpeted hallway and through an arched doorway to a larger ballroom outfitted with marble floors and ornate crystal chandeliers hanging from the domed ceiling. Our footfalls echoed through the empty space, like moving through a museum long after closing.

Another long hallway, the doors on either side all closed, led eventually to an open door and an enormous study. Argus stopped at the doorway, and with a slight bend at the waist, motioned for me to enter with a dramatic sweep of his hand.

I did. He closed the door behind me.

A man slowly rose from behind a large mahogany desk. Somewhere in his middle sixties, he was of average height, with a plump build his expensive and beautifully hand-tailored suit helped to disguise. His dark hair was badly thinning, dyed, combed over and held in place with what was likely a good deal of hairspray. A pair of silver eyeglasses rested halfway down the bridge of his nose.

He looked like an accountant.

"What were you expecting?" he asked, reading my mind. "A dashing leading man in a cape? A monster with pointed ears and cloven hooves? Some deranged madman with an ax?"

"No," I said. "Just you."

"Good to finally chat, Stanley," he said evenly. "I'm Rick Buck."

No one had called me Stanley since my mother had been alive.

"Who are you?" I asked.

"I just told you who I am." His expression remained noncommittal, though slightly amused. "Feeling better?"

I stared at him, saying nothing.

"The nausea will pass, as will the headaches and stomach pains, which can be severe at times. Eventually you'll feel just as you did before."

"Before what?"

"You were awfully sick when we found you out there."

"Out where?"

"Down on the beach, of course." Buck rounded the desk but stayed on that side of the room. Enormous bookcases lined the walls, filled with row upon row of leather-bound books etched with gold leaf. The carpet, like everything else here, was expensive and exotic. Original classic paintings hung in frames on the other wall, lighted from below, and a fully stocked built-in bar, love seat and several classic French chairs rounded out the room. A gorgeous chandelier hung from the ceiling in the center of the room, the light reflecting off the hanging crystals and gold fixtures. "I assume Argus has attended properly to your needs. Are you hungry? You must be. Can I offer you something? I have a fully staffed kitchen."

"I want to leave."

"You're not a prisoner here, Stanley, you can leave whenever you'd like."

"Stop calling me that."

"Isn't that your name?" With a dismissive smile, he strolled over to the bar and selected a glass from a shelf housing rows of them. "Would you like a drink?"

"No."

"Hope you don't mind if I have one." He next selected an ornate carafe of brown liquor and poured a small amount into the glass. Turning back to me, he kept his distance while sipping his drink. "Why don't you join me? We both know you're a man that likes to drink."

I clenched my fists but kept them at my side.

"Oh, come on, Stanley," Buck chuckled. "You're not really going to pull your strong-arm routine, are you? *Here*, with *me*? Really? That fever must've been worse than we thought. You were positively delirious. Must've scrambled whatever's left of those brains of yours. You're lucky we found you when we did. Got you right under a doctor's care. You're welcome, by the way."

"How about we cut the shit?" I said, moving a bit closer.

Buck had another sip of his drink. "Let's do that."

"You didn't *find* me anywhere," I said, spitting the words at him.

"No?"

"You lured me here, brought me right to your doorstep. I saw what you were doing, you and the rest of the freaks in the robes and hoods performing your asinine rituals or black masses or whatever the *fuck* it is you do."

Buck watched me a while without comment. "Well, that all sounds rather silly," he finally said. "As I say, you did have quite a fever, maybe you—"

"People are dead, Buck."

"*Really*? Who? Who's dead, Stanley? Do tell."

I wanted to smash everything in the room. I wanted to grab him by his smug bloated face and pummel him until he was unrecognizable. I wanted to hurt and disfigure him the same as they'd done to me.

"You brought me here, we both know that. So here I am. You're the big man then? The head of all this?"

Something changed in the man's face, a seriousness that overpowered the sarcasm. "Maybe you should be less concerned with who I am and more with who it is I and others like me answer to." He held his glass up and swirled the liquor around as if bored. "It all flows up, Stanley. But you're not thinking about that."

"Rick Buck," I said. "Is that even your real name?"

"Probably not. But do you think it would be that difficult to find out? I'm a prominent, upstanding member of the community, have been for years."

"Who are you all? Who are you really?"

"Who do you think we are?"

"A bunch of sick fucks."

"That's not very nice, Stanley."

"Fuck you."

"We're just crazies who believe in ancient foolishness, who sacrifice human beings, have wild blood orgies and pray to a god long forgotten, is that it?"

"Saturn. You pray to Saturn."

He sipped his drink, shrugged and wandered closer to me. "And where did you get these ideas, Stanley? Where did you get this *oh-so-credible* information? Not one ounce of which you can prove, by the way. From which reliable sources did it originate? Perhaps from some homeless alcoholic that lives on the beach? Or was it the defrocked college professor, the *pederast* who wrote some ridiculous book nobody read anyway? Maybe it was the drug-addicted old bluesman living in squalor on the literal outskirts of town? Could it have been the common thugs and punks who frequent a dive no one cares about or believes is anything other than what it is, an establishment named for the shape and color of the building in which it operates? How about the lunatics and morons with all the conspiracy-theory websites on the Internet? Mustn't forget those bastions of accuracy, authenticity and truth. And then, of course, there's you, Stanley. Just how credible are *you*? An ex-con, a former leg-breaker for low-level bookies and sharks in places like *Revere Beach*, for God's sake. A horrible drunk, a loner and a loser who washes dishes in some greasy spoon, that's what you are, Stanley. And that's *all* you are. But me, I'm a highly respected, wildly successful businessman, entrepreneur and philanthropist. They give me awards. I have plaques touting my humanity all over this house."

My anger was burning so hot I was shaking. "Why did you bring me here?"

"You came to us. It has to be that way so that all things can be completed."

"Why me?"

"Forgive us, but we do have a soft spot for a tarnished soul. One so full of anger and violence, such darkness," he laughed lightly. "Like moths to a flame, some might say. Deep down you've always been just like us, Stanley. Now you truly are." Buck finished his drink, then turned and strolled back over to the bar and poured himself another. "But I have some news. Good and bad, I'm afraid. The bad news is your father has died. His body was found just this morning."

I didn't know whether to believe him.

"My sincere condolences," he added.

"How?" I asked.

"A heart attack, apparently. A massive heart attack."

I remained stone-faced. "Am I supposed to be intimidated?"

"*Intimidated.*" Buck arched an eyebrow. "That seems an odd choice of words. Not saddened or upset or—"

"I stopped giving a damn whether my father was alive or dead a long time ago. If he's really dead and gone, so be it. Good riddance."

Buck smiled ever so slightly. "Well, then the good news should be extra exciting then. Your father left everything to you. Of course, he didn't have much, but he did have the house. It just sold recently, as you know, and although he'd planned to move to Florida and join an assisted-living facility, turns out he hadn't signed the paperwork yet. That means all monies from the sale of the property go to his next of kin. That'd be you, Stanley, and you alone. You just inherited a little over one hundred thousand dollars. That's life-changing money to a man like you."

Could it be true? Could my old man really be dead? Somehow I knew he was, that Buck wasn't lying, and I wanted to feel something besides relief, but that's all I had left in me.

Buck raised his glass. "Cheers."

"So now what?" I asked.

"Go live your life."

If this is real, why did they let me go?

"That's it?"

Why? Why would they let me go?

"Were you expecting something more profound?"

They wouldn't.

"I just walk away? After all this?"

Buck moved back to his desk, sat on the front corner. "You've been marked," he said evenly. "You're ours now, one of us."

I brought a hand to my face. "Why did you do this?"

"You cut yourself," he reminded me. "For *Him*."

My head was spinning again, but my strength remained. "I can't... I...don't..."

"Time's no longer relevant for you," Buck told me. "Run along, go and play, live this life we've given you. We know where to find you. We'll ring the dinner bell when we want you. *We'll* find *you*, Stanley. You don't need to know where we are because we'll always know where you are."

Such horrible sights and sounds crawled through my head, before my eyes.

"The shadows are ours," Buck said.

Blood and horror reflected in a blurred mirror. Dreams of spiders falling from dirty ceilings.

"We reign from within those shadows."

The nausea had returned. My legs began to tremble and my skin turned clammy and cold. I wanted to tear my eyes from my head, to rip my skin and escape my own body and what it was becoming.

"We're the nightmares behind your dreams."

"I'm crazy, aren't I?"

He smiled. "Crazy as hell, Stanley."

"What have you done?" I asked. "What have you done to me?"

"Saved you." Buck calmly sipped his drink. "By giving you life. *True* life."

I knew I had to run, but as I turned to leave, my legs gave out and suddenly I was falling. The room tilted and whirled about like some demented carnival ride, and I collapsed to the floor in what felt like slow motion, only then realizing I'd done so in a cloud of dust, an exhale of The Devil's Breath.

Whoever had been behind me stood over me now, a black smudge looking down at me. And then it came closer, reaching out for me with something in its hand.

A golden chalice filled with blood.

21

I CAN'T SAY FOR sure how long I'd been in the car. Guess it didn't much matter. I knew where we were going, and that's what counted. It was morning but already hot and humid. Despite the temperature, I pulled the gray hoodie I was wearing in tighter around me and watched Sunset pass by the window.

Enjoy your vacation on beautiful Cape Cod!

Behind the wheel, wearing big black sunglasses, her head wrapped in a scarf, Sophie puffed away on a cigarette. In the back, Balthazar lay stretched out in front of the rear window, the seats below packed with our things. We didn't know exactly where we were headed, but away from here, away from this.

Run and play...

But first...this...

I closed my eyes, saw the blood pouring free of that sacred chalice, and those crude drawings of Saturn on his throne in that horrible place where it had all begun. If I listened very carefully, I could hear the music of the rings serenading me from the heavens that surely belonged to him.

We are the nightmares behind your dreams.

The car came to a rather abrupt stop.

It's not sleep you have to worry about. It's waking up.

I opened my eyes. Sophie had pulled over at the end of the road leading to my cottage. I looked over at her and she smiled that wicked smile of hers. I wished I could see her eyes but they remained hidden behind the dark sunglasses.

"Well, go on then," she said.

"Keep it running." I pulled the hood up over my head, stepped out of the car and started toward my cottage. My face was damp and sticky. The wounds on my cheeks had opened again, become bloody.

I wondered if they'd ever heal.

Distracted by visions of my father sitting in his house and preparing to make a phone call any moment now that would distract me from what was about to happen, I quickened my pace.

Time's no longer relevant for you.

No, it wasn't. Full circle, a snake devouring its own tale, coming back around and walking right into myself, that's all this was. Round and round we go, while those in the shadows most don't even believe exist pull the strings.

Somewhere in the back of my mind I allowed a memory of my mother. My poor sweet mother, sitting me on her knee and gently stroking my hair with her fingers, her beautiful sad face smiling down at me as she softly whispered, "It's just a bad dream, little one, just a bad dream."

Dreams that would forever include that oval mirror smeared with blood, reflecting my nightmares, clutched in the hungry embrace of a woman walking across the ceiling like an insect. A mirror that foretold the future by showing me the past, a cloud of concentrated evil and a cup of blood that granted both life and death eternal in a single violent fusion of unimaginable horror and exquisite bondage.

A single exhale of The Devil's Breath.

There's a storm coming.

Albert emerged from the path, returning from his run. He looked at me and smiled knowingly, then continued on without comment.

A terrible storm brewing in those same deep shadows.

Awaiting my touch, the feel of my fingers sliding deep into the wounds on my face as if for the first time, all the while staring directly into my own haunted and suicidal eyes, I walked to my front door, drew a deep breath, and knocked.

AUTHOR NOTE

While this story is of course entirely a work of fiction, the drug known as The Devil's Breath actually does exist, and is potentially every bit as frightening as it is in this fictionalized account. From the moment I learned about it and began researching it, the novel before you began to take shape and eventually became *Devil's Breath*. As always, thank you to Chris, Jess and everyone at Journalstone for getting Devil's Breath back into print with this new edition, and back out to the masses. Also thank you to my wife Carol and to all my friends and family. And finally, special thanks go out to my fans and readers all over the world. I can't even begin to express how much your continued support and belief in my work means to me.

Greg F. Gifune is a professional, best-selling, internationally-published author of several acclaimed novels, novellas and two short story collections. Working predominantly in the horror and crime genres, Greg has been called, "The best writer of horror and thrillers at work today" by *New York Times* best-selling author Christopher Rice, "One of the best writers of his generation" by both The Roswell Literary Review and horror grandmaster Brian Keene, and "Among the finest dark suspense writers of our time" by legendary best-selling author Ed Gorman. Greg's work has been published all over the world, translated into several languages, received starred reviews from Publishers Weekly, Library Journal and others, is consistently praised by readers and critics alike, and has garnered attention from Hollywood. Two of his short stories, HOAX and FIRST IMPRESSIONS have been adapted to film, his novella MIDNIGHT GODS will soon be made into a feature film, and his novel CHILDREN OF CHAOS is under a development deal to be made into a television series. Greg has also served as consulting producer on two films and is currently developing a TV series based on his short story PLANT LIFE and another he created with two colleagues. His novel THE BLEEDING SEASON, originally published in 2003, has been hailed as a classic in the horror genre and is considered to be one of the best horror/thriller novels of the decade. Greg resides in Massachusetts with his wife Carol, a few cats, and two dogs, Dozer and Dudley. He can be reached online at gfgauthor@verizon.net or on Facebook and Twitter. Visit his official site for updates and info at gregfgifune.wordpress.com

www.ingramcontent.com/pod-product-compliance
Lightning Source LLC
Chambersburg PA
CBHW050522260626
47157CB00004B/1430